BOOK 3 OF THE

MANIFEST DESTINY SERIES

THE CRIMSON COMPASS

BETSEY KULAKOWSKI

AND JB CAINE

This is a work of fiction. Names, characters, businesses, places, events, locales, and incidents are either the product of the author's imagination or used fictitiously. Any resemblance to actual persons, living or dead, or actual events is purely coincidental.

Dedication

For all the sisters, both born and chosen.

Contents

Prologue

In the Beginning

Somewhere in the Aegean Sea, ~360 B.C.E.

The sailor raised his weary eyes to the horizon, the sea as black as ink, and the sky just as dark. Only the dappling of stars separated the two. Still, the stars shimmered in the lifting tides, blurring the sea from the sky. Timaeus knew the sky as well as he knew the sea. Both were physical. Both were eternal.

The sailor had plenty of time to contemplate *ψυχή του κόσμου*, the *soul of the world*. It was the intricate connection between all living beings. Living creatures were endowed with a soul and a reason, a mixture of sameness and difference that formed a unified, harmonious entity that permeated the Cosmos. The soul animated the universe, ensuring its rational structure and function according to *The Divine Plan*. It fed the motions of the planets reflecting the deep connection between mathematics and reality.

The Dēmiurgós, the *Creator* ... the One, the Many ... in their infinite wisdom, fashioned and maintained the Universe and its constant rhythm—the heartbeat of everything that lived and breathed, the balance between day and night, good and evil, heaven and hell ... life and death. Same and different. *Becoming* and *Being*.

This fundamental concept challenged reality versus ideals, and tested the teachings of even the great Socrates himself. Plato, his pupil, understood the plurality of gods, though Timaeus was still *becoming*.

He knew the *Dēmiurgós* fashioned and shaped the material world and was as benevolent as any of the gods might be, but he was not sure if assigning good or evil to the *Dēmiurgós* aligned with the thinking of his teacher. Before, there was only chaos, or *chōra*, until *Dēmiurgós* shaped it and constructed the universe as a single, living creature endowed with a *World Soul*, unifying all parts through proportional harmony.

The Divine Plan was not merely an account of the physical creation, but a moral and metaphysical framework that invited human beings to mirror the order of the cosmos within their own souls. Sadly, there were those who refused.

That was why the gods called the Council. They were summoned to discuss a fitting punishment for the arrogance and hubris of those who dwelled with the gods of Atlantis. Once the favored of Poseidon, who founded it and infused it with divine order and law, the god of the sea had been forgotten and the virtue of his people eroded and fell to ambition and greed. And so, Poseidon withdrew his divine influence and left them to their own moral corruption.

Within hours, perhaps minutes, the people would face their judgement at the hand of Zeus, the most high. Poseidon himself had come to Timaeus in a dream and cautioned the teacher and philosopher of the most likely outcome. It had been the sea god himself who gave him the parcel he now kept tucked within his cloak, safe against his heart.

Poseidon had given him calm seas and gentle winds as he spirited away the most sacred treasures of Atlantis. When the earth gave way beneath the island, and the sea took back what it had made, the people would be lost, but their most significant relics would not be.

By the stars, he could tell the lands of Kemet would not be far. There, he would find a people already in communion with the Divine Order of the Universe. His hand went to the pouch containing two objects. Poseidon had warned Timaeus not to consider using either, but he could feel a humming and a heartbeat within, and the sea god's voice had not told him he couldn't look.

Curiosity cursed Pandora, but surely this was not the same. Cautiously, he reached into the layers of his cloak and took out the leather pouch. The cords holding it shut had swollen in the damp air and it was a struggle for his arthritic fingers to pry them open, but when he did, a small object within fell into his hand.

A crystal, as dark as obsidian but as red as blood, swirled with a thrumming tempo that resonated through his bones and into his core. *Lub-dub. Lub-dub.*

The entire galaxy appeared within, swirling like a whirlpool of glistening beauty, as if it had fallen from the very heavens itself. He had to force his eye away.

From the leather sack, he produced an Olivewood box, hand-carved and beautifully made. He studied the carvings, recognizing the double spiral that symbolized the journey inward. One circle for life. One for death. Then there was the star Sirius, the phases of the moon, and the flower of life, a stylized dodecagon.

The *All-Seeing Eye* appeared on the top edge as he studied it. At the latch, there was a carving of a feather crossing a heart. *Beautiful!*

On the back of the box, carefully carved in Greek were the words:

Twelve are the trials and twelve are the truths.

The heart must bear the weight.

The path must hold the light.

By the seas we walk the stars,

By the Compass, find our fate.

Timaeus's hunger to know more got the better of him. His master taught him to seek the answers in all things, and curiosity was the path to knowledge. He fumbled to find the latch, and a large circular piece of metal fell into his open palm. The disc appeared to be forged of *oreikhalkos*—a metal so precious it was considered second only to gold in value. It came only from the mines of Atlantis itself. It reminded him of copper and gold, and it caught the starlight and flashed with the red light of the cosmos. He put the crystal back in the pouch, securing it and tucking it under his arm to protect it as he studied the metallic object.

Turning it over in his wizened hands, he discovered it was a compass, but not just any compass. It was a mariner's compass, but it was a sundial as well. He held it up, turning to find Polaris, the North Star. He held it in that direction and for a moment until he was assured of his position.

Timaeus tapped the Ruby at the center to ensure it was secure, then shook it, trying to make sense of the frenzy. The humming and buzzing from inside the disc increased, and it reminded him of a panicked swarm of bees. Suddenly, he was aware of the rising and falling of the sea, as it increased. Above, clouds gathered seemingly from nowhere.

His small craft, the *Nereide*, shifted and yawed as the wind caught in his white hair and threatened to up-end the craft. He tucked the box back into the bag, tied it tightly and secured it to the single mast.

The clinker-built boat, made of cedar and cypress, waterproofed with pine resin was a sturdy craft, strong enough for solo navigation. It had ample space to store supplies for the voyage. The rounded hull was narrow, but built for speed. The keel was deep enough to navigate rivers, but provided stability in most ocean swells.

Poseidon had given it to him for the journey and it was one of the finest vessels he'd ever seen. The single square sail was made of flax, dyed deep crimson, adorned with the sigil of Atlantis. Dual steering oars were secured, one on each side at the stern, and provided only a small measure of control against the sudden maelstrom.

A wave hit the craft along its starboard side and threatened to toss it into the murky depths. Were the gods angry? Was he not supposed to look? Surely, there could be no harm ...

In a panic, Timaeus stood and lifted his arms to the heavens, spreading them out over the sea.

"Great Poseidon, Lord of the Deep... Father of Islands, Breaker of Ships... hear me now upon your breathless tide," he called. "I am Timaeus, son of Atlantis, lost. I am your chosen carrier of the Compass that turns not to North, but to Fate! I carry the last flame of the Temple! I ask no mercy for myself, only for what I bear. If I must vanish beneath your crown of foam, at least have mercy upon all that is to be left of your once great city, Atlantis! Take me, if you must, but remember my name!"

The sea surged at him from all sides, salt and foam blinding him as he faltered, and lost his footing, stumbling across the deck as the waves dropped out from beneath the craft.

He fumbled the pouch in his panic to catch himself, the contents spilling to the deck as the ship heaved and rolled. The Compass rolled to starboard, the crystal to port. "Poseidon, preserve me!" he cried to the sea, and the dial of brass rolled to his feet. He clutched it into his free hand, pressing it to his chest. As the seas seemed to calm, he said, "Thank you, Sea Father. You have saved me."

But even as the words escaped his lips, a wave lifted, towering above the vessel, dropping atop the deck, sweeping the crystal into a tower of water that lifted it toward the swirling tempest. Lightning crashed around the squall as the clouds parted, opening void to the heavens. He was blinded from all but the brightest stars, but they were not the stars of a sky he knew.

I am betrayed! The words came into his mind as the boards beneath his feet shattered and the craft began to break apart.

"*Mnēsthe tēn Atlantída,*" he cried, as the waves consumed him, ship and all. His desperate plea, *Remember Atlantis.*

1

Shades of Aubergine

East Croydon, London; Present Day

East Croydon Station looked different at night.

Gone were the bustling crowds on the edge of London, replaced by an eerie quiet broken only by an ever-present electrical hum of the overhead lines, the muffled echo of Esme's footsteps on the concrete concourse, and the mechanical voice from the departure board:

"This is the final service of the day to London Victoria, calling at Clapham Junction and London Victoria only. Passengers are advised that there are no further trains this evening."

The harsh overhead lights cast the nearly-empty Thameslink station in a cold blue-white hue, and the few stragglers of the night made their way to the taxi line outside, hoping there would be a cab or two parked there waiting for a late-night fare.

Esme's destination lay farther into the night, and she fought the urge to cross-body her shoulder bag as she turned onto George Street. She fixed her gaze on the spire of Croydon Minster, lit dimly against the night sky. The automatic station doors hissed shut behind her.

The row of bus shelters was largely empty, save for the occasional sleeping tenant wrapped in a stained overcoat despite the warmth creeping into the May air. Wind whipped through the canyon of glassy office buildings and 60s-era concrete block buildings, carrying scraps of litter down the abandoned street.

She felt like she was on display—which, for all intents and purposes, she was.

The air outside the station was cooler, damp with London night mist laced with exhaust fumes and the scent of late-night takeaway. A few buses idled in the distance, and she turned away from them, walking slowly and hesitantly, deliberately looking lost.

She made it two blocks before a figure in a hoodie crossed the road to walk behind her. Esme took note of the stranger, but kept her stride steady. She walked past the flickering neon signs of a still-open kebab shop and a pub.

It felt like every nook and doorway could conceal another dark figure, and her heart pounded. Why had she agreed to this?

She could hear the footsteps of the stranger behind her, keeping pace, then speeding up, then falling into a matching rhythm again. She remembered the Agent training that had *quite literally* been pounded into her over the last six months: *Don't look back too quickly ... check reflections and shadows instead ... breathe ...*

Esme clocked the shadows cast against the buildings by the pale streetlights, confirming that her "company" was fewer than three metres behind her. She'd taken similar walks all over London for the past four nights without incident. Was this it?

She spotted her turn ahead, a narrow road lined on either side with bins and bright splashes of graffiti on the walls between unlit doorways. If this stranger had ill intent, she'd know soon enough. She cut to her left, wondering if he—she assumed it was a *he*—would follow her or continue straight.

The hush of the narrow lane pressed down upon her. A distant car door slammed and she strained her ears to catch soft sounds behind her. There it was: the scrape of a shoe on pavement. If he was going to act, it would be now.

In front of her, a figure stepped out of the shadows, blocking her way. Another emerged from behind the large bin she'd just passed—a classic squeeze play.

"Phone. Wallet. Now."

Esme's hand brushed her bag strap, but she didn't hand it over. Instead, she dropped it on the ground beside her, freeing her arms. Her instructor's mantra flashed through her mind: "*Don't fight angry. Fight efficient.*"

The man in front of her lunged, but Esme sidestepped and spun to her right, driving her elbow into his ribs and crouching low.

The second attacker leapt forward and grabbed her wrist. She pivoted, slamming her knee into his thigh and twisting free, but not completely avoiding a glancing blow across her jaw.

An empathic flicker drove her downward, and another fist sailed over her head close enough to ruffle her hair, and she stomped hard on the first mugger's ankle.

He let out a string of profanity, his voice a bit higher than she'd expected. Teenagers, then? Attacker number two lunged not for Esme, but for her bag.

"I've got it!"

The first man—*boy?*—shoved Esme hard, sending her face first into the brick wall, and the two of them half-ran, half-limped up the alley before turning a corner out of sight.

Esme braced herself against the wall, wincing as she wiped blood from her now-split lip. There was no reason to chase the boys; the purse had been empty except for a few sight-seeing brochures and a couple of rocks. She let out a breath, but tensed as she sensed movement back the way she'd come.

The hooded figure stepped out into the dim light.

Esme groaned. She was getting better at fighting, but she still didn't like it. She pushed off the wall and assumed a kickboxing stance with her fists up and her body at an angle. "Come on, then. Let's get this done." The threatening growl in her voice sounded foreign to her ears.

"I think you've done enough damage here, don't you?" A familiar voice greeted her, and the person reached up and pulled the hood back.

"Wally?" Esme dropped her fists, relief washing through her. "What the hell?"

"I was beginning to think you were one of the least attackable targets in the city. I was afraid I'd have to have a go at you myself," he chuckled.

"You wouldn't have ..."

"Oh, yes, I would have, if those two gits hadn't come at you first. The Order needed you to finish your field testing this week, and I'm tired of hoofing it around London at night." The combat instructor stepped forward and inspected the damage to Esme's face. "Your face is gunna look like a right rainbow tomorrow. We'd better get some wound powder and ice on that lip."

"It hurts." Esme's voice was matter-of-fact, but she could feel tears burning at the edges of her eyes. She blinked hard to make sure they wouldn't fall. "They were just kids, Wally."

"Kids who wanted to hurt you, Esme. Don't forget that. I know this isn't your default setting, love. That's why Solan insisted on a street test instead of just having me sign off on your skills. If you're going to be an Agent, there may come a time when you have to harm an enemy to save yourself. That's just how it works."

"I don't like it," Esme grumped, resisting the urge to pout. Her lip was bleeding enough as it was.

"And that's exactly why it had to be this way. Come on. I've got a car and a first aid kit waiting. I grabbed your bag and tossed it in the boot. Let's get you home."

"I will never like it." She said the words with conviction, but doubt picked at her. Over the last six months, a new version of Esme had awakened. Not *fragile*, not *gentle*. Tough. Daring. Dangerous.

By the time Esme dragged herself through the door of her flat in Westerham, it was nearly one a.m. She paused by the entryway mirror and dropped her purse—her real one this time—on the bench underneath. Her lip had swollen up like a cranberry despite having held ice on it all the way home. She groaned. The crimson and purple bruise blooming along her jawline was a sight, too.

She'd have to cancel lunch with her family tomorrow ... there was just nothing for it. If her sister saw the damage done, it'd do her head in. Eliza knew Esme was in training, but she'd have a proper fit if she knew what the final assessment for that training involved. This would be the third time in a month and, even as flighty as Esme could be, surely her family had to realize by now that she was avoiding them.

She groaned. She turned about-face into the galley-style kitchen and grabbed a bag of frozen vegetables out of the freezer before kicking her shoes off and hauling her sore body into the bedroom. Before she collapsed onto the giant beanbag she called a bed, she made a detour into the bathroom and popped a couple of ibuprofen.

She stripped off her blood-stained shirt and plopped onto the giant cushion.

"You should've seen the other guy," she muttered to the empty room. She pulled the fluffy blanket over her skin, mottled from neck to navel with bruises in various states of healing. She leaned back, gingerly placing the frozen bag against her jaw and lip as she curled up. It would leave a big wet spot on the beanbag by morning, and she'd certainly have to throw the veggies out, but at the moment she didn't care.

Noises from far away, possibly the M25, hummed at the back of her consciousness, but she was exhausted in mind, body, and spirit and chose to ignore them.

Peck, peck, peck. A little bird was pecking at the window. Or was it the door? It was hard to tell.

Oh, but it brought a gift! A shiny ring of keys jingle-jangled, but she couldn't see it because her eyes were closed.

Clever little bird. It let itself inside to bring her the gift. She could hear it hopping across the living room toward her door.

She should probably open her eyes. It was rude not to look at someone or something when it brought you a gift. She should—

"Esme, for God's sake! You were supposed to meet us for lunch an hour ago!"

Eliza's voice jolted Esme out of her dream and she sat bolt upright, forgetting both the state of her undress and the state of her face.

"Bloody hell!" It was her father's voice, harmonized with cries of despair from Eliza and Beatrice. "Esme, what happened? Eliza, grab her a shirt. We're taking her to hospital ..."

"No, no, I'm fine ..." Esme began, but her lip hurt, and the words came out funny.

Eliza was at her side in an instant. "Ez, who did this to you?"

Beatrice picked up the discarded shirt with its crimson stains. "Simon, call the police ..."

"No, no, NO!" Esme insisted. "I'm FINE!"

"You may be many things, young lady," her father began, "but *fine* is not one of them right now! We need to ..."

"We don't need to do anything!" She winced at her own forcefulness and hoped she hadn't reopened the cut on her lip. "I had my final combat training yesterday!"

The other Wrens fell silent for a moment, and the soup of emotions swirling in the air made Esme cringe. Fear, rage, confusion ... too much all at once! Too much! She flopped back on the beanbag and pulled her blanket over her head.

She closed out the sounds of Simon's blustering and Beatrice's questions and focused on the sensation of Eliza's hand on her arm. Esme pictured herself putting her family's emotions in separate drawers, closing and locking each one. When she peeked out from under the blanket, she focused her eyes on Eliza's face.

The Order had been training her mind, too, so that the visions and waves of other people's emotions couldn't wash her out to sea. Eliza was calm. Focus on Eliza.

"Esme," Eliza's eyes were full of concern as she spoke softly, "take a breath and tell us what happened." If she spoke carefully, she could speak in full sentences without coughing. Her progress in voice therapy had been slow but steady.

Esme nodded. "My novice Agent training is pretty much finished now. Last night was my physical test for combat."

"Why weren't we informed?" Simon's voice was low, vibrating with anger.

"Because they didn't test me at the training center." She couldn't bring herself to look at her father's face. If he was angry now, the full truth would put him over the edge.

"Am I to understand that you were given a … a … *field combat test*?"

Esme nodded, still unable to look him in the eye. Eliza wedged herself into the beanbag beside her sister and pulled Esme close, essentially placing herself between Simon and his younger daughter. Esme set her jaw, not because she didn't appreciate the gesture but because being squeezed was *painful*.

"Simon, your blood pressure," Beatrice cautioned. "Don't blow your stack at Esme. She's not a child."

Simon made a noise that sounded a bit like a growl.

"Enough." Beatrice's tone was hard. "There are words to be had, but not with Esme. There's a senior leadership meeting coming up tomorrow afternoon at HQ. I do believe we should invite ourselves to attend."

2

IRON AND ADVOCATE

Eliza stood at the altar, her pulse throbbing in her ears. The perfume of ash and flame burned in her nostrils. The flames of braziers flickered in the periphery of her vision. The blade lay on the table before her, and blood stained the velvet cloth beneath it.

Umbrae vocem audite ... anima fracta, redi ad nos ... Umbrae vocem audite ... Mortui te exspectant.

The translated words rolled off her tongue, muttered in a whisper as dread washed over her. "Hear the voices of the shadows ... broken soul, return to us. Hear the voices of the shadows ... the dead await you."

The din grew louder with every passing day. The voices were a constant presence in her life. When she could keep herself busy, she could ignore them. But in the off moments of calm, when her mind wandered, she could do nothing to drown them out. The same was true for the extremely rare moments when she actually fell asleep.

After two weeks of intense Team Coordination and Leadership training, Eliza was exhausted. It was everything she could do not to fall asleep during supper. As soon as her plate was cleared, she excused herself and retired to her room. Unsure if sleep would find her, she'd picked up the latest Frank Abernathy novel and cracked open the spine. She barely got through the prologue.

She knew she was dreaming. She'd taken Dream Defense and Lucid Awareness training last semester, hoping it would help, but she had yet to master any defense against this particular nightmare.

In the dream, she stood in the last place she wanted to be. The underground temple of the Obsidian Covenant in Dover. It was the stuff of nightmares. Eliza had died here.

Since the real-life encounter with Maelis, she'd died here more than once. She suspected she'd face the same fate tonight. It had become a predictable theme in her dreams. Her nightmares.

"I didn't know this was going to happen," Elias's voice came from behind her. He always said that. Like he hadn't seen it coming. He'd been blind to the powers of the witch who'd seduced him. Their mother always said he wore his heart on his sleeve. It made him vulnerable to the wiles of a seductress like Maelis Varrow.

"You could have stopped it," Eliza said, her voice deep, but strong. She'd wrongly depended upon him to do the right thing when Esme's and Eliza's lives had been in peril. He hadn't.

"No." His voice trembled. "I couldn't."

"You made your choice," Eliza retorted.

"I'd never do anything to hurt you, Eliza. You have to know that."

"But you didn't do anything to save me," she snapped.

"I helped Esme get you to safety, and you know it."

"The only thing I know is betrayal."

She turned around to face him, but Elias wasn't there. She could sense his shadow as it faded, then felt a hand reach over her, grab her by the hair, and tilt her head back. Before she could respond—use the new self-defense tactics she'd been practicing—the blade lifted into her vision, then came down across her throat.

She had visions of Jack the Ripper, but knew it was Maelis Varrow who held the knife. "Eliza Wren, my love." She could hear it speak her name as it broke flesh and hummed with hunger. "We are bound by Death's kiss." It fed on her blood and soul without mercy. Her vision went red.

"This is how it will end," Maelis whispered into her ear as Eliza struggled against her grasp. "Not much longer now."

Others may think you survived, but we know the truth, my darling, the blade seethed in her ears as Maelis lifted it over her head, this time plunging into her chest, scraping against her ribs as it punctured her lung. The blood spurted from her neck, gushing from her chest as the blade came down again and again, piercing her abdomen, tearing her flesh as she fought to block the blows, only to have her arms slashed. Over and over, Maelis ran her through.

Eliza's knees buckled, and she could hear the Chorus laughing. Elias laughing. Maelis laughing. Faces mocked her as her vision blurred. Multiple knives came down on her, piercing her flesh over and over. "Stop!" she cried, pleading. "Stop! Elias! Help me!"

"You're going to die, Eliza," Elias whispered. "Nothing can save you."

"Elias, no," she whimpered. "No."

"You can't escape your fate," he said. "The Shadow of Death is coming for you, and there's nothing you can do."

"Help me ..." she cried. "Elias! HELP ME!" She screamed with a fury and force she hadn't been able to exert over the past year. "Esme! Elias! HELP ME!"

Beatrice raced up the stairs, but was overtaken by Simon, who forced the door to their daughter's room. Faraday was already at Eliza's side, nuzzling against his mistress despite the screaming and flailing.

"Eliza," Simon said, scooping her into his arms, pulling her to him tightly. "Darling girl, you're safe. It's just a dream."

"Mummy's here, darling," Beatrice took over as the screaming dissipated, smoothing down her mousy blonde hair, just as she had when Eliza was a little girl. "Sweet girl, it's okay."

Eliza came out of the nightmare slowly, at a loss for where she was or why her parents were in her room, her cat in her lap. Her hand went to Faraday's head, stroking him as her focus was restored. "What's wrong?" Eliza croaked, her throat sore.

"You were screaming," Simon said. "Was it a nightmare again?"

Eliza didn't answer. Her mother held her at arm's length. "The same one, wasn't it?" Beatrice hazarded a guess, but it was accurate.

"Don't touch me!" Eliza shoved their hands away defensively, her eyes pinched shut, her hair wild about her head.

"I've never heard you scream like that, Eliza Jane." Simon stood and moved to the foot of the four-poster bed. "What does your therapist think about all this?"

"I'm more worried about what her voice therapist is going to say about all the screaming. Did you hurt your voice, darling?"

"Go away! Leave me alone!"

"Oh, dear," Beatrice looked to her husband. "Should I give her one of my valium?"

"Eliza, you need to calm down. You've just undone eighteen months of healing," he snapped, but Eliza wept and bawled even harder until a coughing fit overtook her, turning her face red. Tears rolled off her cheeks, creating damp puddles on her clothes.

"Simon!" Beatrice pulled her daughter into her arms and stroked her hair as tears poured down Eliza's cheeks. "It's not her fault. You shouldn't lash out at her."

"No, but I know who to take this out on," Simon stewed. "Solan should know better than to send untested agents into the field. He's put them through weeks of training. It can't be good for either of our girls. First Esme and now this!? Where does it stop?"

"I'm fine," Eliza grunted, pushing her mother away, sending Faraday scampering. She rolled over and pulled her pillow over her head, her chest heaving beneath the covers.

"No, you're not," Simon snarled. "Both my daughters have been affected by his ... aggressive training tactics! Neither of you has been the same since that whole fiasco with the Veil. I never argued when he hired you for R&D, but this ... this is intolerable! It has to stop!"

"Simon, please," Beatrice scolded him. "You're upsetting her even more than is necessary."

"You think *she's* upset?" Simon balled up his fists. "This is *me* upset!"

Solan Virell never saw it coming. The staff meeting was supposed to be a group discussion with the Board of Directors for the Order, known as the Regents, regarding operations and expansion of the Order's reach into the Americas. The fury of the Wrens was the last thing he expected.

Hell truly hath no fury like Beatrice Wren scorned. She laid into him, her words slicing to the bone. Solan was not someone to cross, but neither were the elder Wrens. Solan sat stock straight, his face a mask of calm contrition as he allowed her fury to burn. "Did you see the bruises on Esme?" Beatrice demanded, her tone razor sharp. She commanded the floor like a barrister.

"It's training, Bea. You remember what it's like," Solan tried to placate her.

"You call it training, I call it negligence. My daughters were thrown into trials that seasoned operatives would hesitate to endure. Eliza left with her throat cut, and Esme left bloodied and bruised like a prizefighter. You think you're tempering them, Solan, but what you've done is broken faith with this family. A family that trusted you. A family that has served by your side for well over thirty-five years."

"We didn't ask any more of them than they could endure," Solan spoke in a tone much lower than his normal, as if raising his voice would only anger her.

"Eliza died, Solan! She may never speak normally again. You took her life and her voice, and I will not allow it. I will be her voice when she has none. *We* will be her voice."

Simon took her hand. "You gamble with our daughters' lives like you own them." He spoke in a measured tone, an iron-willed presence that would not be ignored. His words were few, but heavy as stone.

Solan, for all his charisma, found himself cornered. Still, he didn't flinch. "Don't I?" Solan lifted a brow. "They've each taken their *Oath to the Order*. They serve at the pleasure of the Grand Aegis. What good will come from coddling them?"

Beatrice's eyes narrowed. Simon's hands tightened around hers.

"My daughters are not your pawns," Beatrice stated. "If the Order cannot protect its own from within, then ... what hope do we have against the Covenant?"

Together the elder Wrens stood, staring down the Council, and Solan in particular.

Solan glanced at Charmaine and the Minor Aegis to his left. He gathered his thoughts and stood. "I understand your anger, Simon. Beatrice. But you must know that we would never put your daughters into a situation they could not handle. They're strong and they are resilient, and we are doing everything to support them both and prepare them for anything they may face in this job. I seem to remember Beatrice having a rough go during her training. Or am I mistaken? Was that another agent-in-training?"

"You've missed her entire point, Solan," Simon stated flatly. "Have you learned nothing in the past thirty years? Our girls were not ready and yet you rushed their training. Esme hadn't even completed her final tests before you sent her into the field. Eliza *died* before she even went through the most basic of training. I've hardly seen them these past six months because they continue to go through training after training, when they are clearly still recovering from everything that happened in Romania, and Dover as well. Where does it stop, Solan?"

"Simon, I understand ..." Solan started. The rest of the Council sat watching the exchange.

"Do you?"

Solan moved from his chair and walked over to Simon, putting an arm out. "This is not the time nor the place for this discussion. Ladies and gentlemen, allow us a moment of recess and we'll continue our business at hand. Let me settle this with Simon and Beatrice."

The Wrens didn't want to be removed from the room. They wanted the Council to understand their displeasure. Beatrice knew that Simon only allowed Solan to escort them into his private office because he felt that their mission had been accomplished. While he and Beatrice were more or less retired, they occasionally helped with recon and training when called upon. They also had strong connections to the Regents. Sway, if it was needed. They hoped it would not.

"Simon, Beatrice. Please allow me to offer my utmost regret for the events that have befallen your daughters. As you well know, every mission, every challenge is intended to help a new recruit grow as an Agent. The harder the trial, the stronger the Agent."

"Is that why my Esme is battered? Why her face is bruised and she's moving like an eighty-year-old woman?"

The image made Solan smile. "Your Esme performed most admirably in her trial. You should be proud of her."

"And what about Eliza?" Beatrice asked. "She wakes up screaming from the nightmares that continue to haunt her. All the work to get her voice back has most likely been undone. What about Eliza, Solan?"

Solan's smile faded and his face went stern. "First I've heard of it, Bea. I'll have her dispatched to medical first thing." He picked up his cell phone from his desk and typed orders into the device.

"The girls need a break," Simon stated, sternly. "We're taking them to the manor in Glen Ross as soon as Eliza is cleared to travel."

"Glen Ross? Don't be ridiculous, Simon." Solan rose. "The Amalfi Coast is lovely this time of year. You can have use of my yacht for a couple of weeks. The sunshine and sea air will do more for either of them than some stuffy old manor house in the Highlands."

If Simon was offended, he didn't show it. Instead, he nodded. "That will do."

"I'll have Charmaine make all the arrangements," he said. "You can leave before the week is out."

Simon and Beatrice both nodded and started to turn.

"Eh, Simon, there is one other thing," Solan began, hesitation in his tone. The Wrens paused. "We've tracked down a possible Artifact in Malta..."

"And you want us to see if we can acquire it?" Beatrice snapped.

"What is it?" Simon asked, patiently.

"*Il Sevizio di Mezzanotte.*"

"The Midnight Tea Set?" Simon's brow lifted.

"It's said to have been a wedding gift for a noblewoman, the Contessa Livia Belladonna di Monreale, but she never married. Instead, she hosted many midnight tea parties in the salon of her home, often with ghosts." Simon made no expression. "It's said when two cups are filled with tea, the third is magically filled for whichever lost soul is in attendance."

3

FROM ENGLAND TO ITALY

"I would rather have gone to Glen Ross," Esme complained. "With all these bruises, I'm going to look dreadful in a bathing suit." She draped herself dramatically over the foot of Eliza's bed. Faraday batted at her auburn tresses from under the dust ruffle.

"I don't imagine the salt water will ... do your lip any favors if you manage to re-open that wound, either," Eliza pointed out, her voice barely above a whisper. The gentle, chiding tone came through loud and clear, though. "At least the ... swelling has gone down and it's not so crusty now."

"Ugh. Where exactly are we going again?"

"The Amalfi Coast. Then Malta." Her throat hurt mightily in the aftermath of her nightmare, but Eliza had only recently begun speaking in normal-length sentences again, and she was loath to go back to fragments. A smile played around her lips, something which hadn't happened in ages.

"I suppose that will have its merits. Wait, are you *smiling*?" Esme sat upright, earning a reproachful yowl from the cat. "What do you know that I don't?"

"What? Nothing. Just thinking about ... a holiday ..."

Esme could feel Eliza buzzing with energy, but more importantly, she could see her sister trying to hide the genuine smile threatening to break across her face like dawn. "Oh, my giddy aunt! Is *Phillip* in *Italy*?"

She was referring to Dr. Phillip Thorpe, the brilliant and maverick Order Agent who had been their contact person six months earlier in Romania. She was also referring to the fact that *contact person* had come to mean something very different in Eliza's case where Dr. Thorpe was concerned.

Eliza knew the jig was up. "He might be in Pompeii. He was. I'm not sure if he still is."

"Like hell you're not sure!"

"Oh, come off it, Esme. It's not like we're an item."

"Like hell you aren't!" Esme's eyes were dancing, and her own smile threatened to re-open her lip. "I know you've been talking to him on the regular!"

Eliza suddenly felt self conscious and her smile waned a bit. "A few emails, Ez."

"... and texts?" the younger sister prodded.

"Okay, texts. But ..."

"You *like* him, Eliza. And he's mad for you."

"Oh, he is not ..."

Esme fixed Eliza in a steely glare and pointed to her own head. "You both have been static in my brain since you met. You can't hide feelings from the queen empath."

"You're a fine one to ... give relationship advice," Eliza retorted sourly, feeling defensive in spite of herself. "When did you last have a partner?"

"You know I don't do relationships, Eliza. People have sticky feelings. It takes far too long for me to learn to filter them."

"Oh, really?" Eliza sensed an advantage and an opportunity to turn the conversation away from her own complicated emotions. "What about Liam?"

"One, that was ages ago, and two, that's the perfect example of why I avoid getting involved. I couldn't tell which of us was feeling what after a while, and I stayed with him solidly a month too long."

"Okay, what about what's-her-name from Chelsea?"

"What's-her-name is right. I don't even remember. Nor do I remember the name of that bloke I met at Hever. Or most of them, really. Because *I don't get involved*, Eliza. But *I'm not you.* The only sticky feelings you have to deal with are yours." She hesitated for a minute, then smiled slyly. "And Phillip's. You two are a proper match."

Eliza tried to glare at her sister, but she couldn't help feeling pleased at Esme's assessment. It was true that she hadn't seen Phillip since they'd parted ways six months earlier, but that didn't mean that she didn't still feel the spectral touch of his lips on hers more nights than not. Their emails and texts had been friendly, laced with light flirting, even. So why was she so reticent to acknowledge what seemed so obvious to Esme?

"Okay, fine. I'm hoping that ... maybe we can see each other ... for an afternoon ... before we cast off." Eliza struggled, feeling the damage the prior night's screaming had done to her throat, but refusing to surrender. "And maybe I can learn ... how to operate the boat. The systems are ... fascinating."

Esme chuckled. "Of course that's what you're looking forward to. On a yacht. In the Med. For two weeks." She shook her head. "Heaven forbid you should try to catch some sun or ride a jet ski."

"Maybe a little sun. No jet ski." Eliza shuddered.

"Oh, right. I forgot you were afraid of water."

"Not afraid of the water. Afraid of big things ... I can't see ... in open water."

Esme considered this. "Okay, that's fair, I suppose. But I'm going to ask Solan if one of the crew can get me my Open Water Diving certification. I finished my PADI for Scuba, and I've done some of the Open Water confined environment dives, but the Thames isn't exactly the kind of place you want to certify."

"Why are you ... pushing so hard on ... training? I haven't seen you ... paint in a month."

Esme softened, sensing Eliza's genuine concern. "I'm tired of being seen as *fragile*, Eliza. I want to be able to defend myself. I don't want to feel *helpless* anymore." A haunted look crossed her features, one Eliza recognized well. Esme was remembering seeing her sister's throat cut, watching Eliza's life slip away—and being unable to prevent it. She'd been similarly bound right next to Eliza, her own life in danger as well.

And yet Esme felt guilt for not stopping Maelis's blade.

That guilt should belong to Elias, not her. Eliza leaned forward and hugged her sister. No words passed between them during that embrace, but none were needed.

The cabin lights brightened as the Airbus A320neo dipped below the cloud layer, a glint of golden light reflecting off the Bay of Naples below. Esme and Eliza sat together on the left side of the plane, the senior Wrens across the aisle on the right. To the southwest, the Amalfi Peninsula curved like a sleeping dragon, its cliffs plunging into the cobalt sea. Pastel-colored villages clung to impossible slopes interrupted by terraces of lemon trees.

To the north, rising from the horizon like a myth, Mount Vesuvius dominated the landscape. Esme was struck by the contrast of the vibrant green of the slopes versus the deep rust-red at the peak. Eliza and Beatrice exchanged a pleased look as the youngest Wren's hand absently sketched the volcano.

"It doesn't look asleep," Esme commented. "It looks like it's waiting."

Below the great mountain, Eliza knew, lay the ruins of Pompeii. She had sent Phillip their travel plans yesterday morning, but he hadn't responded. She tried to tell herself she wasn't disappointed—she knew he was working. She just hoped he hadn't gotten himself into trouble by wandering into some semi-stable dig site all by himself. It wouldn't be the first time.

The aircraft banked eastward over the city of Naples and its laundry-draped rooftops, football pitches, church spires, and chaotic streets that looked alive even from 3,000 feet.

"Ladies and gentlemen, we'll be landing shortly at Naples Capodichino Airport…" the British Airways pilot intoned, announcing their impending arrival. In spite of their annoyance with Solan, Simon and Beatrice found themselves smiling, and Esme was abuzz with excitement. She even seemed to have forgotten her earlier embarrassment regarding the multicolored abrasions on her chin and lip. Eliza released a sigh of relief as the landing gear touched down with a gentle but solid *THUMP.*

As they approached the baggage claim, Beatrice spotted a young man holding a sign bearing the name "WREN." She smiled as they made eye contact, confirming their identity. He stepped forward, his smile revealing unnaturally white teeth against his tanned skin.

"Good afternoon. You are the Wren family?"

"We are," Simon nodded, producing from his jacket pocket the letter of introduction Solan had provided. Old school, perhaps, but Solan could be funny that way.

The man took the letter and perused its contents, then folded it back up and tucked it into a leather folio. "Everything appears to be in order. Welcome to *Italia*. My name is Mateo Laskaris, a member of your crew." He wagged his chin at the logo of *The Pleiades* embroidered onto his navy blue collared shirt. "Let us collect your baggage, shall we? I have a vehicle waiting for you, and it will be my pleasure to drive you to the marina. The rest of the crew is preparing for our arrival."

"Thank you, Mateo," Beatrice beamed. "Lead the way!"

After nearly two hours of winding along the Amalfi road, the white Mercedes van pulled into the Porto di Salerno. *The Pleiades's* white hull gleamed in the afternoon sun, and Eliza and Esme caught their breath at the yacht's sheer size.

"All that space just for us?" Esme wondered.

"Yes indeed," Mateo confirmed. "There are three of us on the regular crew. Captain Baxter and Chef Abbot have spent the morning provisioning and preparing your staterooms. I believe Mr. Virell has also arranged for a dive instructor to join us in Malta in a few days."

The humidity sucked the breath out of Eliza's lungs as she stepped out of the van. Still, she took in the lively and peaceful feeling of the marina: the clinking of halyards, the cries of gulls, and the smell of salt and diesel.

It made her feel very far from home.

She followed Esme toward the quay, hypnotized by the light playing on the water.

"I'd recognize that profile anywhere," came a familiar voice from behind her.

Eliza spun around, nearly knocking Esme into the water.

Dr. Phillip Thorpe, his skin darkened by the Italian sun, stood with a canvas satchel slung over his shoulder, wearing a smile that was half-apology, half-challenge.

4

Passionfruit and Peanut Butter

"Phillip?" Eliza gasped, his name coming out in a squeak. "W-what are you doing here?" Her stomach did somersaults and the heat of the Italian summer settled in her cheeks, flaring in her eyes.

"I couldn't let you set sail without stopping by to see you," he said, turning to Esme. "Good to see you again." He surveyed the damage to her lip. "What happened to you?"

"It's a long story. Combat training," Esme blushed, turning to Mateo. "How long until we set sail?"

"The crew are still provisioning the ship and making final preparations. We won't sail til dawn," he said. "The chef is preparing lunch now."

"Why don't you join us for lunch?" Esme invited him. "Have you met our parents?"

Eliza stiffened, panic washing through her. Something about Phillip meeting her parents felt ... *premature*, but there was no help for it now.

Esme saved her the trouble. "Mother, Father, this is Dr. Phillip Thorpe. Phillip, may I introduce Simon and Beatrice Wren, our parents."

"Dr. Thorpe." Simon stuck out his hand. "Pleasure to see you again."

"Simon, call me Phillip." He nodded, then turned and accepted Beatrice's hand. "Beatrice. It's good to see you. You're looking well."

Eliza was stunned. "Y-you know Phillip?"

"We met in Boston a few years ago," Simon admitted.

"Fundraiser for the Peabody Museum of Archeology & Ethnology," Beatrice pointed out for their daughters' sakes. "If memory serves me."

"Your memory is accurate. I hope you don't mind me just showing up. When I heard your daughters were going to be here, I wanted to check in with them. After everything that happened in Romania, I've been concerned." Phillip glanced at Eliza as she averted her eyes and her cheeks pinked up.

"A lot has happened since," Simon said, glancing at Esme. "Come join us for lunch and we'll tell you everything."

The captain met them at the ship and welcomed them aboard. "We were only expecting four passengers." The captain narrowed his eyes, clearly trying to figure out if there were enough cabins on board.

"I'm only staying for a bit, if that's alright. I wanted to catch up with old friends before they set sail."

"Ah, in that case, I'll let Chef Abbot know there'll be one more for lunch," the captain acknowledged. "Welcome aboard."

"I hope you gave better than you got," Phillip chuckled when Esme finished the story of her final exam for her physical combat training course.

"I'm quite sure I did," Esme gushed, proudly. Eliza sat in the corner of the cozy nook on the flybridge, staring at her food, feeling the line of sweat that trickled down her back, madly aware of Phillip's arm against hers.

He smelled of something spicy, that melded with the sea air, and ancient treasures.

"So, tell us, Phillip," Simon asked. "What have you been working on?"

"New discoveries at Pompeii," he beamed. "Some are calling it a once-in-a-century discovery. We found the buried home of a wealthy Roman family that was relatively untouched, completely covered by a dozen meters of pyroclastic flow, preserved for all eternity. There were even loaves of bread that were carbonized, clay pots of red wine that evaporated in the cataclysm." He took out his phone and pulled up pictures from the excavation, handing it over to Eliza. "Scroll through those."

Esme, on her left, leaned in to see as Eliza studied each photograph. The ruins had been reinforced to protect the workers, but the mosaic tile floors and marble columns were remarkably intact. Vases sat on ledges beside voids that looked like small swimming pools. Hot tubs, perhaps. She paused at one in particular. Phillip glanced over. "Isn't it beautiful?" He reached over and took the phone, blowing up the image of an ancient piece of jewelry. It was a ring. The gold was tarnished, but the scales of the two-headed snake was visible as their mouths met as if they were each eating their own tails. The snakes had emerald eyes, the gem stones clouded with age and volcanic detritus.

Eliza took back the phone, her fingers brushing his as he relinquished it. She realized he was leaning against her as she studied the enlarged image. "Marvelous," she muttered, noting details around the snake's heads. Someone had taken great care to polish the ring, but its antiquity was apparent. "It's not *ouroboros*, but it's definitely interesting."

"You know about *ouroboros*?" Phillip asked.

Eliza nodded, but Esme looked confused. "Ouroboros? Is that a brand of Greek yogurt?"

"Ouroboros is a snake eating its own tail. It's an ancient symbol representing eternity, cyclicality, and self-renewal."

"It's common in both Egyptian and Greek iconography," Phillip said, as Eliza passed the phone to her mother to see. "The term *ouroboros* is derived from two words in the ancient Greek language. The first word is *oura* which means *tail* and the second is *boros* which means *eating*. It symbolizes the transmigration of souls, fertility, and in some religions the tail is a *phallic* symbol and the mouth is a *yonic* symbol."

Eliza blushed as she realized what he was saying. She didn't know there was a sexual innuendo hidden in the iconography when she mentioned it. If she'd known, she wouldn't have said anything.

"Fascinating," Eliza's father said, nonplussed as he handed the phone back over to Phillip.

Clearing her throat, Eliza stated, "The German organic chemist August Kekulé described the eureka moment when he realised the structure of benzene after he saw a vision of ouroboros." It was an attempt to redirect the topic back to science rather than something ... awkward.

"Leave it to my sister to make it into something nerdy," Esme scoffed.

"It's not nerdy," Eliza protested, affronted. "It's ... science."

"Nerdy."

After lunch, Esme announced she was going to put on her bathing suit and get some sun. Beatrice excused herself, feigning exhaustion, while Simon announced he was going to go explore the dock before they set sail. Eliza found herself alone with Phillip on the flybridge.

He turned to her and smiled. "So how are you doing, really?" his tone softened and he reached over for her hand. "I'm sorry for how things went down in Zlatna, and I sensed you were struggling, though you never said as much over the phone."

"I'm doing okay," Eliza said, not sure how true it was. "I still have bad dreams, but I saw my counselor and my ENT physician before we left London."

"And what did your doctor say?" he asked, meeting her eyes.

"He wants me to continue vocal therapy for a couple more weeks before he'll consider anything like hyaluronic acid injections or surgery," Eliza said, surprised by how soft his hands were. Archaeologists weren't known for their pristine skin. He was an enigma. "There is some mild improvement, but he reminds me that with an injury like mine, it's more of a marathon than a sprint."

"Wise physician," Phillip observed. "And your counselor?"

Eliza hesitated to answer. She let her hand slip from his, and stood, turning to gaze out across the busy harbor. She noticed Esme settling onto a chaise in her black bikini on the deck below, shadows of bruises still visible on her shins even from this distance. "I won't lie," Eliza finally said. "It's been hard. I almost lost my baby sister. It's affected her, too. She's started obsessing over her physical training because she feels the need to be able to protect herself. I couldn't protect her."

"You can't blame yourself, Eliza. You weren't even there. I couldn't protect her, and I was."

"She isn't your little sister."

"No, but I do have a little sister, and I know how protective that makes you. It certainly makes me over-protective. I'm just thankful Lindsey isn't involved with the Order. She has a nice safe job as an IT consultant and software designer. But I ran off a few boyfriends when she was younger."

Eliza turned back around, considering him for a long moment. She tried to imagine what his sister might look like and envision flashes of Phillip's youth. Eliza had an older brother, and knew Elias might have been equally concerned for her, had he not fallen into the clutches of the Covenant. She still wasn't sure how she felt about Elias these days. He hadn't stopped Maelis from cutting her throat, and she harbored an array of mixed feelings about how everything went down.

"Hey, enough worrying about stuff. How would you like to go into the city for some gelato? I know a place not far from the docks. We can do some shopping or just explore the city, and I'll have you back before the ship sets sail."

Just the thought of a cold treat made Eliza's mouth water. Lunch had been a salad with seafood, and while she was comfortably full, gelato sounded like heaven. "Let me go change into something cooler," Eliza said, glancing at her shirt. She wore the same outfit she'd traveled from London in, and she felt sweaty and uncomfortable.

The gelato was perfect. Eliza couldn't help but read into Phillip's flavor choice: *frutto della passione*. Passionfruit. Eliza chose something less provocative, *burro di arachidi al cioccolato.* Chocolate peanut butter. As they savored their desserts, they walked hand-in-hand along the sea wall, looking out over the harbor below. Eliza was grateful she'd remembered to apply sunscreen, as the brilliant sun made its painfully slow crawl over the western sky. It was still hours from sunset when they would have to say their goodbyes, and Eliza was already dreading it.

Despite her better judgement, she'd caught feelings for this infuriating American scientist. She couldn't deny it any longer. She'd wanted to hate him, to blame him for what happened to Esme in Zlatna and how it had changed her since, but she knew she couldn't. He helped Eliza find her sister and retrieve the missing Artifact. She was thankful for that. Thankful for the gelato, and the quiet companionship as they walked. Thankful for his hand in hers.

"Your voice sounds better," Phillip finally broke the silence, leading her over to a bench. "The Mediterranean air must be agreeing with you." Eliza sat down and was pleased when he sat close beside her.

"Thank you," she said. "I'm still limited, but ... I'm getting there."

"Esme told me the whole story. About your encounter with the Obsidian Covenant."

"Have you been texting Esme, too?" Eliza asked, trying to mask her surprise.

"She reached out to me after you returned to London," he said. "I think she was checking on me as much as anything."

"Maybe making sure you knew she was okay," Eliza thought aloud. "She's a bit of an empath and she might have sensed you needed some consolation."

"Or she knew how much I was missing you," he said. *Oh, so he did miss her.* She knew he was attracted to her, since the kiss in Romania before they parted, but he'd never said as much. "I *have* missed you."

"I've missed you, too," Eliza admitted. "We were just getting to know each other."

"We don't have much time now, but there has been some discussion about me coming to London after I finish this assignment at Pompeii. I wanted to see if you'd be interested in dinner."

"Like ... a date?"

"No," he chuckled. "Not *like* a date. An actual date. If you're interested in that."

Eliza fought back a smile, holding judgment just to tease him. When he leaned in with a questioning glance, and a lifted brow, she let the smile surface. "I'd like that."

"I'll let you know as soon as I know when I'll be there." He sat back and put an arm around her, returning his attention to his gelato.

They ate their treat in companionable silence, not noticing the woman watching them from the balcony of the hotel overlooking the promenade along the coastal wall. She'd been following the Wrens since they arrived, and was particularly surprised by the sudden appearance of Dr. Phillip Thorpe, a known associate of the Wren girls. They'd been spotted together in Romania by one of her colleagues.

Clearly, his interests were more than scientific and beyond the work of the Aegis Order. The affection of the eldest Wren girl clearly had him smitten. The Council of Seven would be most interested in this latest development. American and British agents of the Aegis Order not only working together, but fraternizing after hours.

She continued to watch as they finished their gelato and strolled the promenade, stopping at the many stores and shops offering everything from fresh produce and baked goods to jewelry, apparel, and other necessities. As the day waned and the sun lowered, they stood at the seawall, breathing in the colors as the sun painted the quaint Italian city, nestled on the hill overlooking the harbor, in a prismal spectrum of colors.

Yes, *The Fathers* might find this useful information indeed.

Phillip reached up and brushed a lock of Eliza's hair back behind her ear, admiring the way the flecks of gold sparkled in the fading daylight. "I truly have missed you. I will miss you until I see you again."

She lifted her face as his finger brushed along her jawline. His face was dangerously close to hers. "I'll miss you, too," she admitted. "I hope your work at Pompeii won't keep you long."

"It's hard to say, but we'll call or text every day, okay?"

Eliza nodded. "I'd like that."

Phillip caught her off guard when he leaned in and kissed her. She melted into him, feeling sparks of energy racing through her core. His mouth was tender, but his hand against the small of her back was firm. When he backed away he made no apologies. "I hope that can hold you over for a few months."

"Maybe just one more," she said. This time, it was Eliza doing the kissing.

5

GHOSTS IN THE HARBOR

The air smelled of diesel and the sea, the way southern ports always did in the early afternoon. He'd been positioned carefully since dawn, since the thin line of mist blurred the outlines of riggings and pilings, and he'd watched as the sun crept westward across the brilliant azure sky, bathing everything in a blinding light that focused the world in sharp relief.

Elias Wren crouched in the lee of a storage shed, a small pair of binoculars pressed against his knee, pointed at slip C-12.

The Pleiades. One of Solan's many indulgences—long, white, and smug, even at rest. He'd been following Charmaine for a while now, and he'd overheard her mention Amalfi in passing as he eavesdropped on a morning phone call while in line for coffee at Costa. Her voice had been careful, her tone almost bored, but he'd caught the undertone: *working holiday.* It wouldn't be the first time Solan had toddled off into the Med claiming to be researching or meeting with field teams. And Solan didn't go anywhere without Charmaine.

Elias had followed her around London for three days, sleeping in a rented Fiat and living on take-away. Each night he swore he'd wake up before dawn, drive out of the city, and disappear again. Each dawn he'd stayed.

And now here he was in Italy, having arrived ahead of her, hoping to catch her for a private word before she and Solan took off on another *working holiday*. Certainly she knew by now that Elias was alive, a "*man without a country*," as it were. Dead to the Order, a traitor to the Covenant. And a man who knew too much about the world to simply blend into it as if he knew nothing about secret societies, prophecies, and enchanted Artifacts.

It had been eleven years since he had last seen Charmaine, much less spoken to her, but he could still feel the velvety softness of her skin in his dreams. He'd been an idealist then, a gung-ho Agent in his mid-twenties, throwing caution to the wind by having a secret and torrid affair with a woman four years his senior.

Then he'd died, as far as the Order knew anyway, and she had leaned into her ambition and climbed to what was arguably the second-most important position in the Order, though not with the title and prestige that should accompany it. She'd aspired to be a Regent—the leader of one of the Order's seven divisions—but instead she was Solan's personal assistant.

All the secrets, none of the respect. Elias wondered if perhaps she was working an angle. She usually was, and she played the long game.

He was shaken from his reminiscence by the slam of a car door. A young man in a crisp navy blue shirt stepped out of a Mercedes van and opened the door.

But it wasn't Charmaine who alighted.

It was Eliza. Esme. His parents.

What were ***they*** *doing here?*

His heart hammered against his ribs and his stomach flipped over, filling him with something akin to panic. His sisters walked to the edge of the dock, mumbling to one another affectionately and looking out into the harbor. They didn't see the figure approaching from behind them. Elias crouched lower behind a stack of coiled lines as the man strode toward the sisters.

It took him a minute, but then Elias recognized the man as Dr. Phillip Thorpe, an archeologist from the Artifact Retrieval division of the Order.

Why was he here? And more importantly, why had he approached Eliza and Esme rather than the senior Wrens? Elias hated not knowing what was going on.

There was no sign of Solan or Charmaine yet, and his family's appearance added an additional wrinkle: it wasn't impossible that Esme would somehow pick up on his hidden presence if he didn't back off a bit.

He relocated to a café across from the marina where he could keep an eye on *The Pleiades* from a distance while simultaneously fueling up on good coffee and sfogliatella, a pastry he only treated himself to in Italy. It seemed metaphorically appropriate, the many layers of crispy dough symbolic of the many layers of subterfuge and confusion that plagued his own life. The vanilla and hint of orange blossom water was sweet and gave him a vague sense of hope for his future. He pulled out a laptop and pretended to be working so the shop owners wouldn't kick him out. He kept buying coffee and pastries, too, so they'd have a monetary incentive to let him take up space for a longer time.

He nearly choked on his espresso as Phillip and Eliza passed by the café's large window, hand-in-hand and eating gelato.

Elias felt a pang of something ... jealousy? Worry? Here was this cowboy courting his sister while Elias himself was relegated to shadows.

Night settled over the marina, and Elias had resumed his stakeout spot near the storage shed. He had to risk the possibility of Esme's extra senses in order to offset the guarantee of getting locked outside the marina gates as the hour grew later.

The marina lights scattered over the black water, and Elias found himself nodding off despite the toxic levels of caffeine he'd ingested during the afternoon. A diesel cough broke the quiet, jolting him awake. He looked at his watch, the lume on the dial revealing that it was 2:12 a.m. The marina gate clicked and rattled, indicating that someone with a key had let themselves in the after-hours gate. Footsteps approached, and the long shadows of three figures heralded the early-morning arrivals. Hushed voices mumbled words he couldn't make out.

His ears perked up. The figures passed him, unaware of his presence. *Charmaine.* He didn't know who the others were, but their silhouettes identified them as female. The trio fell silent as they passed by the gangway to *The Pleiades* and boarded a small trawler docked a few slips down. Elias waited for twenty minutes, then crept along the side of a long supply building until he could get an angle on the smaller craft. He pulled out his phone and took a snap of the transom emblazoned with the name *Naxos.*

The first streaks of rosy dawn caressed the water as *The Pleiades* fired up her engines. Elias had climbed a fire ladder to position himself on a roof terrace so he could keep an eye on both her and *Naxos.* He shifted his weight uncomfortably as Solan's yacht slid past the breakwater, turning south.

He was about to move when *Naxos* came to life, following the larger ship from a discreet distance. Charmaine was following. *Why?* The prior day's coffee and carbs turned sour in his stomach. He'd been betrayed by every cause he'd ever served, walked away from everyone he'd ever loved. So where did his loyalty lie now?

He was too lost in his own thoughts to realize he'd been spotted by a man on the ground below.

Several minutes later, Elias stepped off the ladder and shifted the bag on his shoulder, having resolved to make his way to the car and follow the boats' journeys from land. He didn't have to follow Charmaine now; he could still track Eliza's and Esme's phones with his old one, an artifact of a shared family mobile plan from decades past.

One thing about being a man without a country: it instills a proper sense of paranoia.

Elias felt the person following him before he saw the movement out of the corner of his eye. Reorienting away from his vehicle, Elias cut down an alley between two warehouses, the scents of fish and tar thick in the air.

The soft footfalls behind him remained, then quickened. Elias was surprised he could hear them over the thundering blood in his own ears. He broke into a run then, weaving amidst crates and nets, hoping to be able to find a place to tuck away and get a good look at whoever stalked him.

Elias ran toward the water, then doubled back. He'd lost all sense of direction. *Was the gate to the left or the right?*

He ducked behind a wooden fishing boat being serviced in drydock. *Footsteps running*. Whoever it was, they were still behind him.

He pulled an automatic utility knife out of his trouser pocket and deployed the four-inch blade by pressing on the slider. It wasn't much of a melee weapon, but it was all he had other than his own fists and feet. He was miserable at fighting. He needed to get away if he could, but the knife was a last line of defense.

Elias ducked around the bow of the fishing boat—and nearly ran face-first into a stack of pallets. He spun around, seeking some other avenue of escape.

What he found was the angry, dark eyes of one Dr. Phillip Thorpe.

"You're pretty fast for a dead man, Elias."

6

THE CALM AT SEA

Morning light painted the sky in an impressionistic blend of pinks, lavenders, and oranges over the Porto di Salerno, and the western horizon was dappled in the colors of the fading night. Eliza sat with Captain Baxter in companionable silence at the *al fresco* dining table in the stern cockpit. She took a deep breath, inhaling the aroma of espresso laced with the salt and diesel scents of the marina.

The Pleiades eased away from the pier under Mateo's skilled hand.

The beginnings of peace teased at Eliza's soul despite the bad dreams that plagued her every time she closed her eyes. "Captain Baxter, will you teach me all about the boat? What does what, and how to make it behave?"

A smirk tugged at the corner of his salt-and-pepper beard. "Call me Bax." He sipped the last of his coffee and rose. "Every voyage begins with a lie, Dr. Wren. We tell the sea it will behave."

Eliza looked up at him with an expression of half-amusement, half-confusion. "Call me Eliza. Is that a yes?"

He chuckled. "Of course, Eliza. There's a great deal of automation about a boat like this, but you're an engineer, correct?"

"My Ph.D. is in Physics," she allowed. "But I do tend to work in the engineering space, yes."

"You'll want to have Mateo take you through the engine room. I know what all the bits are, but he's a veritable genius with that stuff. I understand what to do if something breaks, but I'm not sure I'd be any good at explaining."

"Fair enough. I suspect there's quite a lot to learn."

"About the technical part, sure. But there's also a certain instinct to being at sea. If you already feel it enough to want to learn, then the instinct is probably in you."

"I'd like to think so," she replied, taking his words as a subtle compliment.

"Come on up to the wheelhouse. Mateo is on shift for a couple of hours, but I'm sure he won't mind the company."

They wandered through the sliding glass doors and the salon of the yacht, navigating a narrow hallway past the galley and into the wheelhouse. Mateo leaned against a tall captain's chair, turning a shining stainless steel wheel to direct the boat out into the Tyrrhenian Sea as pink and gold spread across the rippling water. The first mate nodded as Bax explained the variety of analog and digital gauges on the sleek helm station.

Eliza's mechanical brain thrummed like the massive engines of the boat as he showed her the autopilot system, the radar, even the water temperature gauge that displayed the engine's cooling system. She loved the symmetry and geometry of the helm—the yacht speaking to her not just as a machine, but as a symbol of control over the elements. Something in that gave her a sense of comfort, and she said as much.

The captain shrugged. "Control is always an illusion Dr. Wren—Eliza. You can't fight the sea. You read it, just as you'd read a person. If you're paying attention, it always tells you what it's about to do."

As they ventured into the open water, Eliza scanned the vista before her, feeling very much a part of it—one of a handful of vessels taking to the water in the early morning light while most of the world was asleep.

Behind *The Pleiades* by half a nautical mile, another, smaller boat followed.

The tender nosed into a narrow crescent of black sand hemmed by steep, pine-crowned cliffs. Sunlight poured down the rock face in gold sheets, turning the dark grains of volcanic sand to a shimmer like powdered obsidian. The sea lay glass-green and clear to the depth of the anchor line, its surface broken only by the slow pulse of waves that whispered rather than crashed. A scatter of smooth stones gleamed at the water's edge; farther up, tufts of wild thyme and sea grass clung to cracks in the rock. The air smelled of salt and pine resin, and the only sounds were gulls, the ticking of the tender's cooling engine, and the gentle sigh of the tide sliding up the shore.

Mateo offered a hand to each of the Wrens to help them disembark. Esme caught the shy smile he shared with Chef Amalie as he took the lunch basket from her, then offered her his hand as well. She flushed slightly under his gaze, telling Esme that there was an onboard romance in the making.

"Well, I supposed this might persuade me to forgive Solan just a little bit," Beatrice allowed as she found a dry spot on the beach and spread out a large pale blue blanket edged with a Greek key pattern.

"We will have about two hours here before the tides rise," Mateo began. "There is a much larger beach, but this one can only be accessed by boat or that very narrow trail there," he said, pointing to a small break in the thick treeline, "so you will have more quiet and privacy. Chef Amalie has packed you a picnic. We will go for a walk so that you may enjoy time with each other, but we will stay within earshot. Should you need us, just call out and we will come."

"Thank you, Mateo. This is just what we need." Even Simon's often-brusque exterior seemed to relax in the shadow of the dark basalt and limestone cliffs.

Mateo nodded and set the wicker basket on the corner of the blanket. "We will check in with you in an hour or so. Enjoy this beautiful place."

"We certainly will," Beatrice agreed.

Eliza stared out to sea, marveling as the emerald water turned nearly violet as the depth dropped off. Esme sidled up next to her.

"It's so quiet here," the younger sister mused. "Like everything's holding its breath."

It was such an *Esme* thing to say, at least a pre-kidnapped-by-a-crazy-man Esme, that Eliza's heart warmed. She snaked her arm around Esme's waist in a gentle side hug, still mindful of the fading bruises.

Simon stripped off his linen shirt and shoes, leaving him in a pair of navy swim trunks. "Alright, you two. Last one in is a Scotch egg!" He nudged his daughters as he sauntered into the surf.

"That'd be Liza," Esme laughed, peeling off her own sundress to reveal a brown-and-orange geometric bikini that looked like it belonged in a Bond film. She followed after her father, splashing him as she came up from behind.

"It's almost like that holiday we did in Crete." Beatrice's sudden nearness surprised Eliza, but she didn't jump in alarm as she'd done so many times over the past year. "We're missing one, though."

"Let's just be grateful for this bit," Eliza muttered, not sure if she really wanted to think about Elias and how things used to be.

"Hmmm," her mother agreed noncommittally. "You going to poke your toes in? I'll stay here in the shallows with you."

Eliza entwined her arm with her mother's and they waded out ankle-deep. The elder Wren daughter closed her eyes and listened to the waves making a fizzing sound on the volcanic sand. She turned her face toward the sun, tilting her chin enough that the brim of her wide hat didn't impede the light. Perhaps this was the only way to burn away the terrors of Dover: pure, unadulterated sunlight.

After a light lunch of fresh bread, tapenade, and cheese, Esme produced a sketchpad and pencils from her beach bag. She walked twenty metres up the beach and began drawing the craggy, earthy cliffs that edged the cove. Beatrice and Simon exchanged a pleased glance at the sight of the girl they were afraid they'd lost on a mission in Romania.

"She's more resilient than we gave her credit for," Eliza said softly, acknowledging the thought that had passed between her parents. "Maybe I am, too."

The senior Wrens turned to face her. "What makes you say it that way?" her father wondered, an edge of challenge in his voice.

"Until Niall Roth died in our foyer, we had relatively safe and quiet lives," Eliza pointed out, noticing the tension that rippled through her mother and father at the mention of the murdered man. Was it because of his violent end, or something about the man himself? *Curiouser and curiouser,* she thought, but continued, "Esme and I never sought to be Agents. We weren't trained properly before ending up in the field. Do you think things would have been different in Dover and Zlatna if we'd had more training, if we'd understood better what fieldwork looked like?"

"It might have done," Simon acceded, "but field work is never safe."

"Yet you and Mother have done it for forty years."

"Yes, well ..." He didn't quite know how to respond.

Fortunately, Beatrice stepped in. "Of course, we always want you to be safe, my darling. But if you had chosen to follow in our footsteps, we'd have supported you as we did with your brother. Our problem with Solan, at least on this issue, was that you were plunged into the field completely green, and then a year later, you were put back into the field despite the fact that you still had some months left on your formal training. He should never have allowed such a thing."

"I don't disagree. But what we did ... it was *important*, right?"

"Well, yes, though the world will never know it."

"Are you saying you want to stay on as a field Agent?" Simon's voice was incredulous.

"I don't know. Maybe. I think Esme does. I don't want her out there alone." And by *alone*, she meant *without her big sister*. "Now that we know more, we're better prepared."

A hush fell among them as a future they never envisioned loomed overhead.

Oblivious to their conversation, Esme finished her sketch and looked down at the foamy waves that tickled against her toes, speaking of secrets in a language just outside of her comprehension.

"What are we doing here again?" Corrine sat in the princess seat on the stern of the *Naxos*, a thirty-two-foot trawler they'd rented in Amalfi.

"We're *watching*, Corrie. For now, anyway."

"Yeah, but *why*? You've never dragged us out here to follow that yacht around before."

"It never had the Wren sisters on it before. Having them on that boat creates a situation that needs to be monitored."

"And why is that? And more importantly, why do you feel the need to drag us out here to follow after it with you?" Rhea came up from below deck with a bottle of water in her hand. "If I'm going to be cruising on the Med, I'd rather be able to enjoy it, not sit like I'm on a maritime stakeout."

"Don't be thick. Having Wrens, particularly the 'two turtle doves,' near a Manifest Artifact is serious business. And that *particular* Artifact is part of *our* legacy. Maybe nothing will come of it. But we need to be here in case it does." Charmaine was exhausted by the notion of explaining this extraordinarily simple concept to her sisters *again*.

"You've touched that Artifact half a dozen times and nothing's happened," Corrine pouted. "If it didn't react to you, why would it react to them? They're not connected to this area like we are."

"Not in so many words, but the Twelve Days prophecy hasn't been fully cracked. I'm not taking any chances. Not with them so close ..."

Evening onboard *The Pleiades* hung heavy and soft, a dark blanket muffling everything. The Wren family gathered around a small table on the aft deck as Amalie brought out scallop-shell-shaped bowls of seafood risotto. The comforting aroma of the rice, soup stock, and parmesan rose from the dishes before being carried away on the breeze. Mateo appeared with a chilled white wine and a decanter of cold water.

"The captain will come up shortly to brief you about tomorrow's destination. I hope you enjoy your meal. We will be raising the anchor a little later tomorrow morning, around 8:00 a.m. Breakfast will be available in the salon dining area when you are all up and about."

"Thank you, Mateo," Beatrice beamed. "Today was just lovely."

"I'm glad you enjoyed yourself. Dr. Wren, would you care to join me for a tour of the engine room once we're underway tomorrow?"

"I'd love that, thank you." The thought of seeing the mechanics of a vessel of this size set Eliza's heart aflutter.

"All right, then. I'll have Amalie—Chef Amalie—alert me when you take your breakfast."

"Mateo," Esme spoke, her eyes on the darkening horizon, "what are those lights?"

The first mate looked out to sea and spotted a soft glow. His keen eyes could make out a shape. "I believe that's another boat at anchor, Ms. Wren."

"Isn't that sort of far out to anchor?"

He considered this. "Yes, it is a little odd. The tidal shelf drops off about twenty metres from where we're anchored. They must have a great deal of chain. Still, this is a lovely cove, so ..." His voice trailed off, and Eliza and Esme exchanged a look.

The yacht glided south toward Capo Spartivento, the anchor point for this day of their vacation. While Esme positioned herself on the bow of the boat watching for dolphins and feeling the salt spray against her bare legs, Eliza found herself deep within *The Pleiades's* engine room. It was a mechanical cathedral of hums and heat, and she was impressed by the impeccable cleanliness of the space, gleaming silver and white in the fluorescent light.

Mateo pointed out the generators, the water maker, and the stabilization system. "Everything down here runs because tension is contained. Lose that, and nothing holds."

"Kind of like people," Eliza mused.

"Exactly." The faintest smile touched his lips. "Some of the systems are accessed from panels within the boat itself, of course. The helm controls, a great deal of the electrical and piping, can be accessed if repairs are required. But most everything can be monitored from various stations around the boat. One is here." He gestured toward a small workshop area with a large touch panel near the water-tight door through which they'd accessed the engine room. "There is another at the helm, and some controls on a panel near the galley and on the flybridge."

"It's amazing that all these systems can work together in a relatively tight space," Eliza commented.

"Yes, well, this boat is fifteen years old, so things do have to be repaired and replaced, even if we do regular maintenance. You know what they say about yachts ... buying a boat is like buying a hole in the ocean to throw your money into."

She chuckled. "It's a wonder anyone would do it, then. Particularly if they rarely take the boat out."

"Yes, well, it keeps me employed, so I'm not complaining," Mateo chuckled. "We should be in sight of the lighthouse by now. Perhaps you'd like to go back to the deck?"

"I might go up to the flybridge. I don't care for being too close to the edge."

Mateo studied her for a moment. "Well, you might be in the wrong line of work." His tone indicated that his comment was meant in jest, but it left her unsettled. As she exited the engine room and emerged into the crew quarters, she couldn't help but wonder what the crew knew about her *line of work*.

7

To One's Own Knitting

The coast of Calabria gradually lost its green softness as *The Pleiades* approached Capo Spartivento. The pines thinned out, giving way to stark limestone cliffs hued in shades of pale honey and creamy white. Eliza caught her breath, her heart hammering against her ribs.

White cliffs.

White cliffs look so pure, Eliza thought, *but cliffs like that—they take things.*

She shook her head, chiding herself for falling into Esme-like thoughts. She shouldn't personify things this way. The rock ahead of her was just that: rock. She mustn't think of such things as *alive.* She ran through its chemical composition: calcium carbonate, often in the form of calcite, with trace elements of iron carbonate, clay, and quartz. She knew how such rocks were formed: a sedimentary rock formed of shells and the skeletal remains of marine organisms, cemented together over millions of years.

The science of it grounded her, steadied her heart. She'd have to remember to tell her therapist how well it had worked.

The pale cliffs caught the sunlight like blades, and above them the lighthouse appeared—a sentinel at the edge of the world. Just a pinprick in the distance now.

Eliza's reverie was shattered by the unexpected buzzing of the phone in her pocket. She drew it out, and nearly dropped it when she saw the sender's name.

Elias.

She took a pinched breath and punched the screen. He hadn't texted her from this number in more than a decade, though she had certainly left her share of text messages and voicemails on it.

I know where you are. Don't trust Solan.

Pent-up rage gritted her teeth. How *dare* he open a conversation that way. Did he have them under surveillance? He had no right ... She thought carefully before responding.

Are you watching us? Where are you?

She thought she could get more information out of him if she contained her anger.

Let's just say I'm not too far away. But I mean it, Eliza. Don't trust him. He's trying to win your loyalty with flashy gifts.

My loyalty is won by actions, not gifts.

It was a subtle dig, but it made her feel better to hurl it at him.

This isn't about us. Naturally, he caught her meaning. She supposed he must have listened to her messages. ***Solan can't be trusted. He has been hoarding Artifacts for his own benefit for years.***

The accusation surprised her. *How would you know that?*

If you want proof, search his private cabin.

What is it you expect me to find, Elias?

He has an ancient compass on board. The Order doesn't know he has it. It's supposed to keep the ship from sinking.

How. Do. You. Know. This?

I can't explain right now. But you'll find it. And maybe a little trust for your brother, too.

Eliza lay in her berth, wide awake, despite the gentle rocking of the boat. The room was dark. Her cabin was on the seaward side of the ship, so no light reached her small windows. Sleep remained elusive, despite her exhaustion. She spent the entire day with Captain Bax and the First Mate. It left her mind awash with thoughts of engine components, navigational systems, and ocean currents. She tried to picture the seas moving around the craft and feel the pull of the ship against its anchors.

It was easier to obsess over the trivial things. It kept her from thinking about things she'd rather forget. *Elias.*

The nerve of him, texting like that! Accusing Solan of something as absurd as hoarding relics. Solan was the Grand Aegis. He'd taken the same Oath of the Order she and Esme had taken. But then again, so had Elias. Or had he? She thought surely he must have, but maybe that was just an assumption on her part. She'd never heard anyone say otherwise.

Besides, Solan couldn't be hoarding Artifacts. There were too many checks and balances for such things. *Relic Recovery & Management 101.* She'd sat through the three-day webinar that might have been a cure for insomnia had the professor not been so interesting: Randall Greaves, the Senior Archivist for the Order.

Of everyone she knew in the Order, Randall was probably her favorite person. After all, she let him keep her cat when she had to travel. Faraday got along famously with his cat Tiberius, but also with Randall himself. If anyone was a good judge of character, it was Faraday. Besides, the Archivist knew his stuff, and the first two hours had been a lesson in the history of the differences between Aegis and the Covenant and how they approached Artifacts.

Aegis: preserve, protect, prevent use.

Covenant: obtain, observe, offer up for use.

The two organizations would never agree on the basic philosophy of the Artifacts or what to do with them. That's why the Order had rules. They applied to everyone, from the top down and the bottom up. Even Solan. *Especially* Solan.

Damn his eyes! What was Elias trying to accomplish? Why did he know where she was?

Where was he? What did he care? He was a turncoat on both sides.

Benedict Arnold to the Covenant.

Judas Iscariot to Aegis ... and to Eliza.

Eliza startled when her phone chirped.

You should be sleeping. It was Philip.

How do you know I'm not?

You texted me back. Damn. He had her on that one. Cheeky bastard. She didn't text him back though. She lay her phone on her stomach and ran a hand over her weary face. *Damn his eyes, too.* Those beautiful, deep brown eyes. A girl could get lost in eyes that dark. Her phone chirped and hummed again, ringing this time.

"Hey," she answered softly, afraid she might wake the whole ship.

"What's going on?" Phillip's voice was equally warm and gruff at the same time. "I'm worried about you."

"Why?"

"You're not sleeping."

Eliza shrugged, letting the phone rest on her shoulder. "It's nothing new. I didn't sleep well even before Zlatna."

"What about Dover?"

Eliza hesitated, caught off guard by his boldness. "Wait, how did you know I'm not sleeping?"

"Little bird told me," he said

"A little *Wren*?"

"Your sister is worried about you."

"My sister needs to stick to her own knitting," Eliza muttered under her breath.

"I can help ... if you're open to hypnosis."

"Why wouldn't I be open to it?"

"Some people see it as little more than smoke and mirrors."

Eliza knew his credentials. He wasn't a neurobiologist or a psychiatrist, but he had an interest in alternative medicines. She'd learned that about him in the last six months.

"Do you know a hypnotherapist?"

"I dabble in it," he said. *Of course he did.* "Are you lying down? Lights dim?"

"Yes," Eliza shifted in her bed. Settling.

"Close your eyes and listen to the sound of my voice." Phillip began, softening his tone, his own voice deep. "I want you to take in a slow, deep breath, five ... four ... three ... two ... one. Let it out slowly. Five ... four ... three ... two ... one." He repeated this several times. "Now focus on your body. Start at the top of your head and allow each muscle to tense and then release. Into your neck. Your shoulders. Your arms ..." This continued till even her toes were relaxed. "Imagine a ball of white light swirling above you, spiraling down around your body. You can feel it against your skin as it moves around and through you. It's warm and fills you with a sense of peace. Let go of all your cares. Let it melt your worries. Focus only on the sound of my voice. You're safe and you are not alone. There is nothing you need to be. Nothing else."

No, there was nothing else. At that moment, he was everything, and the memory of his lips on hers, his hand in the small of her back, came flooding back. She forgot everything, succumbing to the magic spell he cast over her, not even aware she'd nodded off to sleep.

One minute, she was lying in her bunk; the next, she stood outside Solan's private cabin. Her hand hovered above the doorknob tentatively. Solan's trust meant everything to her, and this felt like a violation. She was almost relieved when the door didn't open.

Of course, it would be locked. Perhaps she suspected it. She hadn't come ill-prepared. She had a small tension wrench and a pick in her pocket. She knelt at the door and inserted the tension wrench into the lower part of the keyhole, gently twisting just enough to feel the levers press back. Using the pick, she probed for each stack in the lock.

The room was dark, except for a dim line of accent lighting built into the woodwork. It gave the room an amber glow. The woodwork appeared to be highly varnished, and the cabin was as luxurious as the rest of the vessel. There were sofas covered in cream leather. An oriental rug on the floor was soft against her bare feet. A compass, huh? Eliza moved to the desk, scanning the items on its surface before her eye went to the built-in bookcases with glass doors. On a ship, everything had to be designed to keep objects in place. In rough seas, the last thing you wanted was your precious tchotchkes to get tossed around.

Solan had books, expensive books. Leather-bound, antique tomes. What appeared to be a handcrafted model ship took up one whole shelf.

She moved in for a better look, determining it was the *HMS Victory*. There was an antique globe in the middle of the shelf, but above it, she found what she was looking for.

The Compass wasn't anything spectacular. It was metal. Probably brass. It had an aged patina and was heavy when she brought it down and set it on Solan's desk.

Umbrae vocem audite ... anima fracta, redi ad nos ... Umbrae vocem audite ... Mortui te exspectant.

The voices came from nowhere and everywhere. Eliza froze, a shadow in the darkness. "Who's there?"

Umbrae vocem audite ... anima fracta, redi ad nos ... Umbrae vocem audite ... Mortui te exspectant.

Eliza pressed her hands over her ears, trying to deafen herself to the voices. "Stop it! Go away! What do you want with me?"

"Eliza," her sister's voice found her, and a ghostly figure resembling her sister, standing in the corner behind Solan's desk, came into focus. "You're dreaming. Wake up."

"No," Eliza said. "I'm not. I can't sleep."

"Eliza," Phillip's voice found her. "Are you okay?"

Eliza opened her eyes, and realized Esme stood over her in her pajamas, hair disheveled. "Eliza?"

"Phillip," Eliza sat up, pressing the phone to her ear. "I have to go. I'll call you tomorrow." She hit the red button ending the call.

"What the hell was that?" Esme demanded.

"Did you text Phillip and tell him I couldn't sleep?" Eliza countered.

"Well, yeah," she said. "Don't think I didn't notice how you pine for him."

"I wasn't *pining* for Phillip," Eliza grumbled, now on her feet.

"Oh? Really?"

"No," she snapped. "But that's also not the point."

"Then let's get to the point. Are you going to tell me what you were doing in Solan's office?"

"I wasn't in Solan's office," Eliza was still trying to figure out what had happened. Had it been a dream? Then it hit her. What Esme had done. "How did you get into my dream?"

"You're not the only one who knows how to *pick a lock*."

8

FALSE CALM

Eliza sat in the dining area on the flybridge, a cup of tea going cold in the darkness just before dawn. Esme had gone back to bed, but Eliza was too restless to sleep. In the east, a dark mountain glowed red, and puffs of clouds circled it. Vesuvius was north of Sorrento, so this had to be Mount Etna, Eliza decided.

It had been over a month since the latest eruption of Mount Etna began, triggered by a fracture at the base of the Bocca Nuova crater. Etna made Eliza think about Vesuvius and Vesuvius made her think of Pompeii. Pompeii made her think of Phillip and Phillip made her think about her bizarre dream and Esme's odd reaction to it. Having him call in the middle of the night was unexpected, to say the least, but somehow, she felt like Esme had manipulated him to put her in a state of hypnosis, and it'd allowed her little sister to get into her head. She knew Esme had visions, but she had no idea her little sister could astrally project into someone else's dreams. It had to have been a set up, Eliza was convinced.

The distant rumble of the earth made the water ripple as a wave rolled past the boat, now anchored in the harbor. The sky glowed brighter and

Eliza's sense of curiosity got the better of her. She pulled up her phone and did a quick search.

The National Institute of Geophysics and Volcanology reported that ongoing explosive-effusive eruptions at Mt. Etna had decreased, but there were still episodes of Strombolian explosions from the Southeast crater. She was no geologist, but knowing that eruptions were decreasing provided her some measure of comfort. It was bad enough that she didn't like the water—or the creatures living in it—but she didn't like the idea of a volcano blowing its top while she was anywhere near it. Still, the glow had to be from lava rising from a vent on the mountain's upper slope. It was still too early for sunrise to be creating it.

Then, Eliza made the mistake of checking the status on Vesuvius, where Phillip was working. She'd assumed the website would tell her that the volcano was dormant or extinct. She hadn't heard of it doing anything since Pompeii was destroyed, so Phillip would be safe from an eruption. Or would he?

In the past fourteen days, Vesuvius had recorded over 400 earthquakes of magnitudes up to 4.9. But no eruptions. She tried to convince herself there was no need to worry as she reached for her tea, despite it being cold.

"Dr. Wren," Amalie appeared from the galley. "You're up early."

"Couldn't sleep," Eliza said. "I helped myself to a cuppa. I hope that's okay."

"Of course," Amelie said. Eliza liked the young French woman. She wore her brown hair cropped short, her curls tucked behind her ears. Eliza had been impressed with Amalie's prowess in that small galley, feeding them all some of the most amazing dishes Eliza'd ever had. "Are you hungry? I just put some orange scones in the oven. I'll bring you a plate as soon as they come out."

"Thank you," Eliza said, realizing her stomach was a bit grumbly this morning. "That would be nice."

"Do you take coffee? Or is the tea sufficient?"

"Tea for me," Eliza said. "My parents are coffee drinkers."

"Noted," Amalie said. "I just need some supplies from the lazarette beneath the seat cushion." The woman went to the bench seat across from where Eliza sat and lifted the cushion, revealing a storage area beneath. There, she had her dried goods stored. Plastic storage containers filled with bags and boxes of flour, cereals, rice, and pasta filled the void.

"I never would have thought to check the cushions for a snack," Eliza chortled.

"Storage on a yacht is always at a premium," Amalie said. "I have an extra refrigerator and freezer below deck aside from the combo unit in the galley, and every inch of empty storage space goes to non-perishables and necessities. By the time we get to Malta, I'll be running low on fresh produce; fortunately, there's always a good selection at the market in Valletta."

"I do enjoy a nice farmer's market," Eliza sighed with a deep breath.

"You'd be welcome to tag along," Amalie said. "There's more than just produce. It's a terrific international market with all kinds of textiles, pottery, jewelry, and hand-crafts."

"I might have to take you up on that," Eliza nodded.

"I'll let Bax know you're in," she said, gathering the supplies she'd found. "I'll bring you a tray of scones in just a bit."

Eliza thanked her and turned her eyes back to the horizon, and the glow that now emitted from low in the sky. That was the sunrise, she decided, glancing at her watch. It had to be.

Esme rubbed her weary eyes as she climbed up the steps to the flybridge, finding Eliza with a pot of tea and a table full of food. Eliza was nibbling on a scone. "I thought you'd sleep longer," Esme fussed, sliding into the booth beside her, reaching for an empty tea cup on the sideboard as she passed. Eliza took up the kettle and poured her a cup. The perfume of cinnamon, mint, ginger, and orange wafted from the hot liquid. Esme recoiled.

"Don't knock it til you try it," Eliza said, sensing her sister's hesitation at the unfamiliar blend. "Amalie tells me this blend is called *Evening In Sorrento* and it's the most popular Italian tea."

"I didn't know Italians even drank tea," Esme sniffed and took a tentative sip of the hot liquid.

"The other option was called *Romeo and Juliet*, which is green tea with papaya, rose petals and strawberries."

"Well, we know you won't opt for that one," Esme scoffed. "How can you not like papaya?"

"I don't know, but every time I've ever had it, I didn't care for it."

"You're just weird." Esme snatched up a scone with one hand, and reached for a handful of strawberries with the other. She was too tired to worry about table manners. She ignored Eliza's look of displeasure as she reached for the jam.

"Dr. Karitzotis in the physics lab says I'm eccentric," Eliza said. "I think I'd rather be weird than eccentric."

"Dr. Karitzotis is eccentric," Esme said, shoving food into her mouth.

"I tend to agree with you," Eliza laughed, taking up her tea, "and he smells like mothballs and licorice."

"Ew," Esme cringed. "I never got that close to him."

"Lucky you," Eliza smirked.

Eliza sat back, nibbling on her scone watching while Esme made an absolute pig of herself. She'd gone rather thin over the last year, and it was heartening to see she had an appetite, but it wasn't pleasant to watch. Their mother would have thrown a fit if she were here.

"I've seen Mother eat like this before," Esme said with a full mouth. "So don't judge."

"Excuse me?" Eliza furrowed her brow. "First you walk in on my dreams, now you read my mind? What's gotten into you? Has this new Esme Wren given up any of the civility she was raised with?"

"It wasn't like I meant to walk in on you. You were the one astrally projecting," Esme scoffed, dropping her scone, sitting back in her seat. "I was happily enjoying my own dreams until you started wandering about. Why were you even in Solan's private office?"

Eliza set her jaw and stared down her sister as her heart thundered beneath her blouse. She didn't want to tell Esme about the text messages from Elias, but then again, if anyone needed to know, it might be her sister.

The internal debate raged on for what seemed like a full minute before Esme spoke up. "What are you not telling me, Eliza?"

Eliza opened her mouth to speak, but the words wouldn't come.

"Eliza ..." Esme's tone was challenging as she dragged out her name.

"I ..." Eliza started, but stopped. "You can't tell Mother and Father."

Esme looked like she might refuse, but then softened. "And why not?"

Eliza's brow knitted. "Because they don't need to know."

"Know what?"

Eliza stared down her sister, debating, but then took a deep breath. "Elias."

Esme's brow shot up like Mr. Spock's on *Star Trek*. "Elias? What does he have to do with anything?"

Setting aside her tea cup and pushing back her plate, Eliza glanced around to make sure no one was within earshot. "He texted me."

It took a moment before Esme responded. "Well, that does bodge things up a bit, doesn't it? Why would Elias text you? *How* would Elias text you?"

"I've had his old number in my phone all these years. When I miss him or I'm angry with him, I leave him a voice mail or send him a text. It's more of a way for me to vent, because I know there's no way ... I mean I *thought* there was no way he could possibly still have that old number. But apparently I was wrong."

"Wait, he texted you from his old number? Surely Mother and Father took him off the family's cellular plan when we thought he died."

"One would think," Eliza said. "If I say anything now, then they'll have to and I don't want to be left without some way to reach him."

"After what he did? Why do you care?"

"Because he told me something I can't believe, and I have to think at some point he'll need to know how wrong he is."

"What did he tell you?"

Eliza clammed up again. Esme gave her a challenging glare. "He said Solan's been hoarding Artifacts. That there's one here on the yacht. In his office."

Esme let out a gasp. "You were spying on Solan? To see if Elias was lying?"

"No!" Eliza snapped. "*I* was dreaming. *You* were the one spying on *me*."

One point to Eliza.

"Eliza, darling," Beatrice found her daughter reading in her cabin. "We're going ashore. Are you ready?"

Eliza glanced up, and blinked slowly. "It's time already? Yes. Yes. I'm ready." Eliza folded her book shut and rose from the chair tucked into the corner.

"Were you sleeping, dear?" Beatrice took a step into the room and inspected her daughter.

"No," Eliza said defensively.

"You look tired, darling."

"Don't I always?"

"You need some sunshine," Beatrice said. "And wait until you see the tower at Palazzo Corvaja and the theatre of Taormina."

Eliza wasn't accustomed to being a tourist. The island of Taormina was beautiful and the ancient sites were fascinating. She tried to figure out how they were built in a time when modern construction techniques weren't a thing.

"The city is known as the *Pearl of The Ionian Sea*," Eliza heard one of the tour guides speaking English to a group of tourists outside a trattoria where the perfume of baking bread had her attention.

She was relieved when her father announced this would be a perfect place for lunch. It had been a long time since the scone and fruit she'd had for breakfast.

Esme ordered the au gratin mix of calamari, prawns, and swordfish sprinkled with almonds and pistachios. Her father chose the fresh catch of the day, tuna, while her mother went with an Italian version of a salad niçoise. Eliza finally decided on the Sicilian *busiate* noodles served with shrimp and pesto.

The food was delicious, the bread fresh from the oven, and Eliza couldn't help but eat everything on her plate. But Esme was finished before Eliza.

"I think I'm gonna go ahead and check out Mount Tauro, if no one minds," Esme said.

"Go along," Simon nodded. "We'll follow when we get done. I'd like to be back down before sunset."

"We thought we might have a glass of wine at Bar Turrisi at sunset," Beatrice said. "Captain Baxter said it was one of the most beautiful spots on the island to watch the sun go down."

"Did he tell you about the decor?" Eliza asked. She'd read the local tour guides online before they left London. The bar was famous for their bizarre Greek decor that might be defined as risque at best. Greek stone phalluses were nothing shocking to scientists, though. *Seen one, seen them all.*

Eliza yawned and pushed her food around after Esme left.

"Poppet?" Her father was staring at her when she looked up. "Are you okay?"

Eliza lifted a shoulder non-committally. "Just tired."

"Maybe you should go back to the boat and lie down," Beatrice suggested. "You could meet us for cocktails later."

"I was hoping to see the view from Mount Tauro," Eliza said, then let out a sigh. "Take pictures for me?"

"Of course, dear," Beatrice said, reaching over and taking her hand. "Go rest. We'll be in Syracuse tomorrow and you'll want to visit the ruins there, I'm sure."

Simon folded his napkin and laid it beside his empty plate. "I'll go take care of the check."

As soon as he was gone, Beatrice picked up her purse and fished around for a bottle. "Here," she opened the bottle and took out a pink pill, laying it in her daughter's hand. "Take this."

"What is this? A sleeping pill?" Eliza recoiled, pushing her hand toward her mother, prepared to drop the medication back into the bottle.

"No," Beatrice said. "It's Benadryl. I used to give you these when you were little and couldn't sleep."

"You drugged me?"

Beatrice looked affronted. "I did what I thought was best ... under the advice of your pediatrician."

"Mother, I'm not five any more."

"You've never been able to rest well, and I hate to see you suffer like this. Take it. It'll help quiet your mind so you can sleep. Worst case, you won't have to worry about whatever pollen they have here in the Mediterranean. Might help your red eyes."

Eliza sat for a moment with the pill in her palm, then surrendered. "Fine." She tossed the pill into her mouth and washed it down with the last swallow of her sparkling water.

Her parents went on to follow after Esme as Eliza headed back down toward the coast. But instead of going to the yacht, she detoured through the cobblestone streets and found an interesting little boutique filled with antiques of all kinds. The owner greeted her in Italian, "*Benvenuta*." The old woman smiled a toothless grin. Her hair hovered over her head like a cloud, but barely covered her scalp. "*Entra. Entra. Posso aiutarti a trovare qualcosa?*"

"Oh, I'm sorry. I don't speak Italian," Eliza said, but understanding she was welcome to come in.

A man's voice echoed from the back of the shop. "*Mamma, lei non parla italiano. Parla inglese al turista!*"

"Ah, English, sì sì. What you find? I help you look?" the old woman managed, her smile never fading.

"Oh, well. I just wanted to look around," Eliza said.

The man must have translated as he walked to the front of the store. The woman smiled and patted Eliza's arm, returning to the checkout area. He met her as she strolled down the first aisle, which was narrow, the store crammed with all manner of things. "Apologies," he said. "Mamma's English isn-a so good. Please, let-a me know if I can-a help you find-a anything."

Eliza's eye had already been drawn to something on one of the shelves. He noticed her look and he reached up and took the small wooden box and handed it to her. "Are you a jeweler, *Signorina*?"

"No," Eliza blushed as she studied the small tools inside the wooden box. "Nothing like that."

"A cat-a-burgler then-a?" He winked at her with a mischievous grin. "Perhaps-a locksmith? These are-a the tools-a of-a the trade-a."

"Oh, heavens no," Eliza realized what he was implying. "I'm an engineer by trade. But I have a fascination with clockworks." She thought on her toes. "Are you saying these are for a locksmith? I was thinking how helpful they'd be for setting gears and sprockets in a small clock. They're so delicate."

"Si, si. I could-a picture that-a," he said. "For you-a, miss, only €85."

Eliza hesitated. She hadn't meant to buy anything, but the tools reminded her of the dream. She knew if she was going to get a look at what Solan had in his office, she'd need the right tools for the job. Everything she'd seen on the ship had been much too large, and she'd left the small screwdriver set she'd bought to fix her glasses in her bedside table back in London.

When he saw her hesitate, he softened. "Seventy five-a?"

"Could you go lower? I don't have much cash on me and I left my bank card in my room." It was a lie, but she had two €20 banknotes tucked into the outer pocket of her wallet. She reached into her wallet and drew out the bills. "Could you do €40?"

The man glanced at the money, then his eyes darted to the tools before his gaze lifted to her. "You are quite-a the negotiator, Miss. Si. I can-a do €40, I ask-a just one favor."

"What's that?"

"Walk-a the entire store, look-a at everything, it-a makes-a my Mamma's heart-a happy when-a people come-a to visit her. You pay-a her when you are-a ready to go-a, okay?"

Eliza stuck out her hand. "Deal." The man grinned and took it, shaking her hand vigorously.

She was halfway back to the boat when she came to realize she'd waited far too long to return. The Benadryl was more effective than she expected and she wanted to find a quiet park bench and curl up on it to go to sleep. She was tempted to get a coffee, but she didn't really like coffee, and she never drank energy drinks. Besides, that would be counter-productive. Instead, she pushed through and finally made it back to the docks, surprised to find Captain Baxter in the water beside the boat, with a mask and snorkel.

"Are you inspecting the ship?" Eliza asked, when she realized it was him.

"Checking for barnacles," he said. "Besides, it's so hot, I thought the water might feel refreshing."

"Are barnacles a problem?" Eliza didn't know anything about barnacles, but as part of her engineering education, she surmised that would be a normal preventative maintenance check.

"Yes, of course," he replied. "Barnacles create drag and that affects fuel consumption, sometimes as much as thirty to forty percent. I felt like the engines were straining, and I have found some, but not many. I was about to go check the propeller too. Sometimes they get tangled in seaweed or other detritus."

"Can they damage the hull? Barnacles, that is." Eliza leaned on the rail watching as he worked.

"Sure," he said, "and though most of the time it's cosmetic, it can corrode metal parts such as the propellers, shafts and hull fittings."

"See, I learned something new," Eliza said, shouldering her bag.

"If you see Mateo, let him know I've got it covered. No need for him to gear up and come down. Looks like we'll need to check the fuel filters after all."

Eliza nodded and went on her way, finding Mateo as she boarded the ship. She conveyed the message. "Ugh, I was hoping to avoid the fuel filters. It's a messy job and I'll smell like diesel fuel for a week."

"Sorry," Eliza said. "Captain Baxter sounded equally disappointed."

"It's a complicated process," he said. "Wanna help?"

That was tempting. She was still tired, but the last leg of her walk had given her a second wind. She might not sleep for a while. "Sure," she said, glancing down at her skirt and her sandaled feet. "Let me go change."

"I'll give you some overalls to wear, so your clothes don't get dirty, but you still don't want on your best outfit."

The smell of diesel hit her in the face as he opened the hatch. The engine had been off when Eliza returned, so at least it'd had a little time to cool since they arrived in port long before sunrise. Mateo climbed down and turned back to offer a hand. Then he wedged himself into the narrow engine bay. The Racor filter gleamed in the beam of his torchlight, the clear inspection bowl had gone cloudy with grit. "There you are," he muttered to the Racor, not to her. He glanced back at Eliza. "Do you see that?"

"What am I looking at?"

"The glass bowl allows us to see the fuel. If it's clean amber, that's good. What do you see?"

Eliza bent over to take a good look. "Looks mostly clear to me," she said. "What's all that in the bottom of the bowl? Looks like tea leaves in the bottom of a teacup."

Mateo laughed. "Will you read my fortune, Dr. Wren?"

Eliza put her hand to her forehead and let her eyelids flutter as her eyeballs rolled back. "I see a new filter in your future."

"Well done, Dr. Wren," he said. "That's most likely a build up of debris or sludge in the fuel. We'll tap this small petcock valve and drain the fuel in the Racor then I can pull the filter. Once we get a look at it, we'll know for sure if it needs a change."

He did, and then announced, "Oh, yes, Dr. Wren. A new filter is in order."

A twist of the drain valve and a thin stream of brown water ran into the catch pan. He replaced the filter cartridge, hands slick with fuel, the smell permeating the cramped quarters, adding to Eliza's euphoria as the Benadryl kicked in again. When he hit the primer lever, the pump made its steady click-click-click until the fuel ran clean again.

"Now, let's go see how we did," Mateo turned, just as Eliza pitched forward. He caught her before she could tumble into the dark void below.

Mateo sat at the helm taking the chewing out he knew he deserved. Baxter's face was as red as Simon Wren's and he couldn't even look at Beatrice.

"What do you have to say for yourself?"

"I was working even lower in the engine room than she was," Mateo finally got an opportunity to speak. "It wasn't oxygen displacement or hydrocarbon vapors. I'm sure of it."

"Were there any confined space entry protocols implemented before you made entry into the engine space?" Simon demanded.

"The engine room has a forced ventilation system," Mateo said. "I double-checked its functionality this morning because I suspected the fuel filter would need to be changed. Captain, I told you so when we made port this morning."

"What did the doctor say?" Baxter turned to Beatrice.

"He's examining her now," she said. "Her pulse ox was 96.8% but her blood pressure was low."

"See," Mateo stuck out a hand like that explained everything. "If it had been O_2 deficiency her stats would be much lower."

The doctor appeared from Eliza's quarters below, his face placid. "How is she?" Baxter asked, not waiting for him to say.

"She's a-sleeping," he said in a thick Italian accent. "Apparently, someone gave her Benadryl, and she's particularly susceptible to it, I'd wager."

"I gave her Benadryl," Beatrice admitted. "She doesn't sleep well, and I thought it might help."

"On top of exhaustion and dehydration, yes, this is not abnormal then," he said. "She needs to sleep and rest. No shopping. No climbing these hills." He waved his hand in the general direction of the coastal city. "Bed rest for the next forty-eight hours, at least. Three to five days is better."

"That is why we're here," Esme scowled, chiming in for the first time. "My sister doesn't understand the words *rest* or *relaxation*."

"She better learn," the doctor said. "When do you leave for your next port?"

"Tonight," Baxter said. "Syracuse tomorrow before we head to Malta."

"My sister is a physician in-a Malta. I'll give you her number. She can-a follow up when you arrive."

9

The Compass Awakens

Eliza was still moderately grouchy the morning she woke in Malta. Late the night before, Bax had dropped anchor in the Grand Harbour of Valetta. She'd been quite literally coerced by her family and the crew to do nothing but *rest* for the past two days, and while the scenery was among the most beautiful she'd ever seen, she was bored out of her mind.

She'd also been under everyone's watchful eye and hadn't been able to make use of her lockpicks to prove once and for all that Elias was wrong about Solan.

Probably the only thing that had kept her from a one-woman mutiny was Amalie's constant supply of snacks, including the chef's gift of a box of Jaffa cakes from her personal stash.

She was preparing to go out to breakfast when a quiet *tappity tap* on her door, which she immediately recognized as Esme's whimsical knock, interrupted her morning ablutions. She pulled her cabin door open and eyed her younger sister with a poorly-hidden scowl.

"Oh, Eliza, you must stop being cross with me. I was trying to help you."

"By dream-crashing, Ez?" They'd had echoes of this same conversation at least three times during Eliza's convalescence.

"I told you, you weren't dreaming. You were projecting."

"Enough, Esme. You know I don't do things like that. That's your department."

"All right, that's it. We're going to sort this out right now. And you're going to listen to me with an *open mind*, Liza. It was fine for you to be all pouty and snarly the last couple of days because I know you weren't well, but this projection thing is serious. Denial of the fact that you projected doesn't make it less true."

Eliza blinked. She wasn't used to Esme being stern with her, and it surprised her enough that she sat down on her berth and crossed her arms. "I'll listen to what you have to say, but that doesn't mean I'll agree with you."

"That's a start, anyhow," Esme sighed. "You're partly right in that this is usually my area of expertise, and as such, my Order training has included coursework on a variety of psychic skills, some of which I have, and some which I don't. Turns out that I do have a very limited ability to project my consciousness, which is sort of a wonky extension of my empathy. I'm not much good at it, but I've probably accidentally done it a few times in my life and written it off as a dream, just as you're trying to do."

Eliza chewed on her lower lip but remained silent. Esme took this as encouragement to continue.

"Right. So projecting isn't really all that uncommon, as it turns out. What's hard is doing it on purpose. But it's quite different from dreaming in that there are actual safety risks."

At that phrase, Eliza's ears perked up. "Such as?"

"Such as getting lost, Eliza. Normally, your spirit is essentially elastic-banded to your body. So in an actual dream, if you fly off on an astral journey, you're going to make it back just fine as long as no nasty spirit manages to jump into your—"

"Wait, what now? That could happen when I sleep?" Eliza was well and truly alarmed now, and forgot to disbelieve in the concept of astral projection.

"Don't twist your knickers. It's extraordinarily unlikely because there are sort of natural protections against that. But what happened to you is different."

"Different how, exactly?"

"Because *you weren't sleeping,* Eliza. You were *hypnotized.* Which is really just a deep and suggestible form of relaxation—"

"I know what hypnosis is, Esme."

"Of course you do. But the point is that you were awake and suggestible at that moment, and for whatever reason, your spirit felt like it wanted to go on walkabout and check out Solan's cabin, even though you didn't consciously make that decision. And unlike a dream state, you're not tethered to your body the same way. So when you started making noises—"

"I made noises?"

"Yes, you were singing or spouting poetry or something. So Phillip texted me and asked me to check on you. *Which I did.* And it's a good thing, too, because thanks to my coursework, I knew what was happening. So I reached into your mind so I could be your tether and guide you back."

Esme's certainty eroded Eliza's doubts, and it occurred to her that she might actually have been in danger. She certainly hadn't realized that anything was unusual until Esme had materialized in Solan's cabin. "Wha-what if I hadn't been able to find my way back?" Her voice was uncharacteristically small.

"Then you'd have become unsure of what was real and what wasn't, and the longer you were stuck, the more confused you'd be when you came back. Maybe for a long time."

"Oh." Eliza's eyes were wide. "I, uh, well ... thank you, Ez."

Esme let out a deep breath. "You're welcome. Now stop being a sour-puss. You're out of the brig today! Amalie mentioned something about a farmer's market. You could go with her as long as you don't overdo it."

"Wait, where will you be?"

"Bax is going to drop the tender and take me to Cirkewwa to meet my dive instructor, remember? I have my first open water dive today!"

"Oh, that's right. And Mother and Father are going to get that tea set."

"Exactly. And Mateo and Amalie are going to get provisions at the market. So you can go buy flowers and fruit, and whatever else your little heart desires."

As tempting as a good farmer's market was, though, Eliza had the stirrings of a better idea of how to spend her morning.

"Oh, poppet, I'm so sorry to hear that!" Beatrice cooed over her elder daughter. "I feel just awful for giving you that Benadryl. I've spoiled your holiday." Her eyes were awash with guilt.

"Mother, don't be silly," Eliza consoled her. "It's just a lingering headache. I'm sure I'll be right as rain after a little bit of a lie-in today. Perhaps I can join everyone for lunch?"

The Grand Harbor of Valletta glowed in the early light. Golden limestone walls reflected the sun's rays toward the line of white luxury yachts that bobbed at their moorings. Breakfast was a light continental, and Amalie had laid out an array of fruit, breads, sliced meats, and cheeses.

"You see there, pet? She'll be just fine. She's just being sensible. We'll all run our morning errands and then reconnoiter for an afternoon of sightseeing!" Simon was in unusually high spirits, and looked affectionately at Eliza before popping a fat muscat grape into his mouth. "These are absolutely brilliant!"

Beatrice sighed. "Your father thinks he's on a mission today," she said conspiratorily to the girls. "Let's not ruin his fun."

"Well, it is a mission, after a fashion," Simon went on, unperturbed. "We are retrieving an Artifact, are we not?"

"In the most technical sense, yes, indeed." His wife didn't add the clarification that they were simply going to an antique shop where the tea set was on hold under Solan's name. All they had to do was pay for it and pick it up.

"I'm certain that Solan will appreciate you're running this erra—ahem, I mean *mission*—for him, Papa," Esme grinned.

Beatrice and Eliza gave muted giggles, but Simon's mood would not be dampened. "Esme, what time will your dive lesson be finished?"

"Should be done by half twelve, I think, but then the dive instructor's going to drive us back. The training center is all the way on the north coast, so Captain Baxter is going to take me up there in the tender and drop me off. The dive instructor is going to stay aboard for a few days so I can get some supervised experience and finish my certification this week."

"Excellent use of your holiday, my dear," Simon approved. "Bea, my love, shall we be off?"

"I suppose so. Not that there's any hurry but your own excitement," she chuckled. "But I suspect I can persuade you to walk hand-in-hand with me in the gardens?"

"No persuasion needed, dearest ..." They gave an absent wave to their daughters as they wandered away from the *al fresco* dining area in the ship's cockpit.

"They're acting like they're schoolchildren," Eliza quipped, but with a smile.

"Yes, well, we should all be so blessed," Esme replied fondly. "I must be off as well. Bax will be ready to take me in a few minutes. Enjoy your *nap*, Eliza." Her tone indicated that she knew Eliza had no intention of sleeping at all.

It was everything she could do not to hurry to Solan's office as soon as Eliza saw Captain Baxter motor away with Esme in the tender. Afraid he might return for some odd reason, she waited an ungodly thirty minutes—plenty of time for her to panic, but not enough time to talk herself out of it—before she took her lockpick kit from the storage locker under her bed. The boat was cloaked in an eerie quiet while at anchor. The only auditory evidence that Eliza wasn't actually in a building on land was the soft slap of gentle waves against the side of the yacht.

She took the few steps to the door of the owner's cabin and knelt, rather surprised that the lock was exactly the one she'd seen in her dream, or vision, or projection, or whatever the bloody hell it had been. She remembered that there were six levers she'd have to nudge along until the bolt slid free and was grateful that she wouldn't have to rush. In the back of her mind, it registered that having a lock like this on an internal cabin door in a yacht was *definitely* a safety hazard in case people needed to abandon ship in a hurry. She shook the thought away and bent to her task.

The tension wrench slid easily into the keyhole, and Eliza pulled a small pick with a bent end out of the tool wallet. She gently maneuvered the pick through the succession of levers until she felt each one catch until the bolt clicked free and she could unlock the door. It only occurred to her after the fact that she wouldn't be able to relock it. There was nothing for it now, though.

Eliza didn't have to look around for more than a nanosecond to realize that the cabin was exactly as she'd seen it before. She made a beeline for the glass cabinet with the *HMS Victory* and looked on the shelf above it.

There, below the globe, was the bronze object she sought. It wasn't a compass in the modern sense; it more resembled the antikytheras of ancient Greece. Rather than an arrow on a magnetic dial that skewed to the north, this object was a hexagonal casing around a series of concentric dials with Greek symbols and hashes marked in mathematical precision. In the center there were prongs that looked rather like a jeweler's setting, and Eliza wondered if some other device was meant to be affixed in the center. She shuddered to think how old this Artifact might be.

She shuddered again when she realized that the presence of this device in this location meant that Elias was right. Something was rotten in the state of Denmark. Or the city of London, rather. And that something was Solan Virell.

"It is important not to be nervous," the dive instructor, Niko Stavros, said in a calm deep voice. The thick Greek accent added to the allure of this creature who appeared to be the very image of Apollo himself. He wore a skin tight, knee-length, short-sleeved dive suit that clung to every rippling muscle in his perfect body. The zipper wasn't fully drawn, and she could see the dark mat of hair that ran up the middle of his tanned and chiseled abs.

"I'm not nervous," Esme said, the lie rolling off her tongue with an unnatural ease. "I spent hours in the dive pool back home to get ready for this." If she was nervous about anything it was *him*. She hadn't expected her dive instructor to be so hot.

"A pool is one thing," he pointed out. "The ocean, no. It is different."

"How long have you been diving?" Esme asked, trying to gauge his age. It might have been close to Eliza's, but he could also be much older. It was hard to tell with him looking like a tasty snack.

"I've been diving all my life," he answered. "I joined the Hellenic Navy as soon as I was old enough and earned a spot with the Special Forces where I trained with the United States Navy in Counter Mine Operations and Submarine Search and Rescue. I've been a master dive instructor for over twenty years."

Military. Of course. That explained a lot. But *dammit*, that meant he was much older than he appeared. "Wow," Esme managed, not sure what else to say.

"Look, Miss Wren," he said, his tone soft and encouraging. "I have more dive certifications than any other dive instructor in the Mediterranean. It is my job to ensure you are successful in obtaining your certification this week. My first concern is for your safety. Today's dive is a test of your basic abilities, but it is not your final exam. I wish to help you become accustomed to diving in an ocean where safety is not guaranteed. You will become confident in your own abilities so you can manage any challenges you may face."

Esme nodded, suddenly at a loss for words. Niko turned his back toward the beach and pointed out toward the open water. "See where the water goes from light to dark? There is a reef there, and just beyond it, the shelf drops off to about fifty metres. We will begin with a tour of the shallows, just to get your buoyancy control device properly adjusted, then go out over the reef and down, maybe twenty to thirty metres. Sound good?"

"Sure," Esme swallowed hard. "Easy peasy."

"Then let's get you equipped. Do you have a dive suit?" his hand went to his perfect chest.

"No," Esme said. "I figured I'd get one here."

"Then we will go into the dive shop and you can pick one out," he said. "Your entire week's dive and all equipment have been paid for in advance."

"Oh." That didn't surprise Esme. "Brilliant."

Esme fitted her mask to her face, her fins still in her hand as she sank beneath the warm water. Her buoyancy control device—or BCD, as Niko called it—fit over her wet suit like a vest, her oxygen tank, and regulator attached to it. Niko strapped a dive computer to her wrist making it look like a watch. He instructed her on the parameters of the dive and how to read the gauges. She'd already been instructed on these things back in the dive pool at the Aegis Headquarters, but she didn't say anything.

"Diver one, radio check," his voice came through the earpiece attached to her mask. "Copy?"

"I can hear you," she said. "We didn't have these fancy speakers in our masks back home. I like it."

"Keep the protocol, Miss Wren. Mic check." He sounded annoyed, but the amused grin behind his mask told her it was okay. He explained the protocols to speak in short, clear phrases, no slang, or long explanations, and to always end with *copy*.

"Not *Roger*?"

"That's a military-affiliated response," he said. "In the civilian or commercial setting, we use *copy*."

"*Copy* that, Diver One. Diver Two responding. I hear you loud and clear. Copy."

She could see Niko's smile behind his mask as he donned his flippers. "Visibility is about ten metres. Water temperature is approximately twenty-one degrees celsius. It's a good day for a dive."

He was not wrong about that.

The water was luminous. Sunlight rippled in threads across the sandy bottom. Esme could hear her own breath through the full-face mask, each inhale drawn through the regulator. Each exhale a slow hiss of bubbles. In the pool she'd struggled to slow her breathing so she didn't suck down her oxygen before her bottom time was up, but somehow the beauty of the sea—and her handsome and confident dive instructor— calmed her.

"You're doing great, Miss Wren. Nice and easy. Keep your fins level." Niko's voice found her as a school of bright colored fish darted up from the reef ahead.

"Copy that," Esme responded. "It's beautiful down here."

Niko didn't answer, but pointed to the coral ridge. A school of silver jacks flickered and vanished behind the shelf wall. Twenty metres out, the sea floor fell away. The water grew darker and cooler. Niko pulled ahead, his strong kicks giving him more thrust than hers. Esme paused, too, to check her pressure gauge and her BCD, realizing her buoyancy was keeping her from descending. She made an adjustment and found herself thrust forward much easier with the next kick, though the current pushed her sideways.

She felt a sharp tug at her shoulder, suddenly no longer moving. She kicked again, feeling a sharp sting in her leg. *Shark?* Panic settled over her as she realized how much further away Niko was. He couldn't reach her in time. "Help!" she gasped, struggling, now certain a shark had her. With every kick, pain shot through her leg. "Help! Niko! Something's got me!" Her mind raced into threads of irrational thoughts. She tried to twist around to see what the problem was, but the motion pulled on her mask and water leaked in. Her pulse quickened, but she exhaled through her nose, expelling the water from her mask.

"Stop moving." She realized Niko had reached her, as he grabbed the front of her BCD vest. "You're snagged."

"Help me! I'm caught." Her words came faster, chopped by breathless panic.

"Listen to me," he caught her mask in his hand and turned her panicked eyes to his. "Breathe slowly. Deep breath in, then a long slow exhale. You have plenty of air. You are not in any danger." God, his eyes were so blue, even at this depth. "I got you. Your regulator hose is snagged on the coral. I'll have to work it loose, but I don't want to damage the coral."

Niko reached over and found her hose hooked over the jagged outcropping. "Am I bleeding?" Esme thought she saw blood in the water.

"Just a scratch," he said. "The coral will do that. Let's go down to twenty metres and practice maintaining that level for a few minutes. I have a first aid kit with my gear. I'll tend to those when we get back to shore." Esme tried to hold her leg where she could see the scrapes, but her mask and the equipment made it difficult to see.

Twenty metres below, Esme steadied herself at the bottom of the abyss. It wasn't entirely dark, as beams of light shone down from above. Niko hovered a few yards away, scanning the coral shelf. "Hold here," he said. "Just enjoy how beautiful this reef is."

Esme did. Everything felt still. Almost too still. Then, without warning, something shifted. It was subtle at first—a soft tremor through the sea. It felt like a heartbeat rather than a sound. The currents tugged at Esme's hair, lifting her body from the bottom. Tugging against her tank. The ocean wrapped its arms around her, holding her as something came for her, drawing her into a darkness from which she could not escape.

Down, down the ocean drew her, deep into the murky depths. Toppled stone columns seemed to rise from the sea floor, a paved roadway between heaps of rubble which had once been structures. She found herself in a temple much like those she'd seen while sightseeing on the journey. An altar stood in front of a statue, a sea god of some kind, though in the dark it was hard to make out the details. A large shell rested on the stone altar, illuminated with a beam of light that cut through from the surface. She realized the shell was a vessel, holding a gemstone that sparkled and cast rainbows through the temple. The facets were sharply cut, maximizing the luster of the deep red stone. *Ruby or garnet*? She thought to herself.

"Miss Wren?"

"Niko?" Esme's voice sounded panicked even in her own ears. "What's happening?"

"Take a breath," he said. "You're fine. Check your dive computer. How much air do you have?"

"My air is fine," she snapped, as the school of jacks swirled around her like a silver tornado. "Something pulled me down."

"It's just the current," he soothed. "We've been down here for—"

"It's not the current," she insisted, her eyes lifted to the surface that was still painfully far away. A dark shadow passed between her and the sunlight. Panic became the tempo of her heartbeat as she struggled for the surface, searching for a safe escape route. "Niko!"

"I'm right here," his voice found her, and she realized he had a hold of her ankle. "You can't surface faster than your bubbles. You could suffer from decompression sickness."

Esme realized she was free from the vision that had gripped her. She relaxed and forced herself to hover, her eyes scanning above for any sign of sharks, but found none. "I'm okay," she said more to herself than to him, trying to calm herself. "I don't know what happened."

"Panic can do that to you," he said. "I think that's enough for today. Let's head back in."

In the time it took for them to reach the beach, pack up their equipment, and catch a ride back to *The Pleiades*, Esme began to piece together what must have happened. Eliza must have gone for the Compass. Alone on the yacht, she had the opportunity, though Esme had doubted Eliza would have the courage to do it. Her sister could still surprise her once in a while. Esme hadn't been the only one to grow a little moxie over the past year or so. Could her taking possession of the Compass have triggered *something*?

10

AUTOPILOT

"All right, out with it," Esme insisted as she slipped into Eliza's cabin after dinner. "You've been twitchy all day. You barely ate, and you've had that really awkward fakey smile on your face every time anyone looks at you. Did you find it?"

"For goodness sake, close the door!" Eliza hissed.

"Oh, there's no one in the hall. Relax!"

"Relax? I've just burgled the Grand Aegis, Ez."

"So you found it then?" Esme's eyes sparkled. Apparently the moral quandary was lost on her.

Eliza sighed. "Yes, I found it."

"Well?"

The older Wren sister got up off the bed where she'd been sitting questioning her life choices and retrieved an object from her hanging locker. It was wrapped in one of her shirts.

"Just bundled it up in your washing, did you?" Esme teased.

"Well, I figured no one was likely to go digging through my dirty clothes," Eliza shrugged, handing the wadded shirt to Esme.

"Good grief, it's heavy!" Esme unwound the fabric to look at the object within. "What does this do?"

"Don't fuddle with it, Ez! We don't know what it does or what will happen if you shift the dials! If it is an Artifact, doing anything at all to it might have consequences." Eliza sat down next to her sister. "Are you picking up anything from it?"

"Nah, I'm only touching your shirt. Nothing at all going on there." Esme smirked at Eliza, who squnched up her eyebrows in response. "Something happened on my dive today. I think this had something to do with it." Esme set the Compass on the bed and laid her hand gently on one of the six flat sides. "

Immediately, her eyes took on that milky sheen they often did when she fell into a vision.

The sea, always the sea. Where everything begins and ends. Esme tasted the brine of the ocean on her tongue, felt the prick of salt air on her cheeks.

Floating on the tide, like flotsam from a shipwreck, then sinking ... sinking ... down into the open arms of Mother Ocean.

Esme watched as the light from the surface became more diffuse, only a pinprick of light like watching a shooting star from behind.

She came to rest gently on the sandy bottom and lay in peaceful silence for a heartbeat—or was it a lifetime?—as the silhouettes of distant fish passed above. Reluctantly, she turned her attention to what was around her on the sea floor: toppled stone columns seemed to line a paved roadway between heaps of rubble which had once been structures.

Rise, *she told herself.* Rise above the vision. See what came before.

In the back of her mind, she remembered the training the Order had given her to help control her visions. She extended her arms like a bird spreading her wings, and she began to float back to the surface and could survey the sea floor from above.

Yes, a road, a long one. A ghostly image of the past appeared over the landscape like a photographic double exposure. A handful of buildings wavered in the superimposed vision, and as Esme rose higher and higher, she could see that the road led to a city surrounded by a circular wall.

Then her spirit broke the surface and was hovering over the sea, still rising like Icarus toward the sun.

"Blast it!" Esme shook herself free of the vision and turned to a very startled-looking Eliza. "I lost control before I could see everything, but I did pick up a few things." She told Eliza what she had seen.

"I've never seen you in control of a vision at all!" Eliza's tone sounded like praise, and Esme grinned.

"I'm getting better, right? No more seizures! No more passing out!"

"Well, that's a relief. It will be nice not to find you crumpled up in the garden again." She gave Esme a wry smile. "Sounds like you saw the Compass's origin."

"Yeah, but I can't shake the feeling that something was missing, though. Like I was only seeing part of the picture." She picked up the Compass and handed it back to Eliza, leaving the shirt in a heap on the duvet.

The moment their fingers brushed a sharp current leapt between them. For an instant the women, the cabin, the whole world seemed to hold its breath. The relic in their hands was no longer sleeping.

With the Compass tucked safely away, Eliza ushered Esme off to her own cabin, lest someone find out what they were up to. She felt like a child who had snuck a peek at her Christmas presents, afraid that her parents would pluck the fact from her brain by simply reading her guilty face.

She lay in her berth, staring at the ceiling, then out the window, then back at the ceiling for hours. Had she been able to fall asleep, she might not have noticed the sounds or the anchor chain, the rocking of the boat, or the near-frantic sounds of movement on the deck above.

Confused, she rose and put on her robe, then headed straight for the bridge.

"I don't *know,*" Mateo was insisting as she entered.

Captain Baxter was rubbing his eyes, clearly having been freshly awakened.

"What's going on?" Eliza asked. "Are we changing marinas?" Both men turned toward her, their faces contorted with befuddlement bordering on panic.

"Well, that's a good question," Bax grumbled, shooting a look back toward Mateo.

"I'm telling you, I didn't do anything! It's like the boat is on autopilot."

"What are you talking about?" Eliza stared at Mateo, knowing that what he was saying was impossible.

"I'm talking about the fact that I was just doing a late-night check of the power usage, and suddenly the anchors raised themselves and the boat started to move. *That's* what I'm saying."

"So we're adrift?" Her voice was incredulous.

"Not exactly," Bax answered, studying the nav panel. "*The Pleiades* is taking us somewhere, but none of us are driving."

"How is this even possible?" Simon demanded. Baxter and Mateo both looked at him blankly.

Eliza added to the inquiry. "From a physics or engineering standpoint. Explain how this is possible. Are yachts like this equipped with autopilot?"

"Well, yes, of course," Baxter said. "Autopilot systems can act like a silent crew member, but there are limitations. We never use them in port. Someone still has to be at the helm to avoid other boats and stationary obstacles. It works like the cruise control in a car. Also, something raised the anchor."

"But not like a Tesla," Esme stated. It wasn't a question.

"No," Mateo said. "It relies on waypoints and chartplotter systems—GPS."

Baxter scowled, shaking his head. "When activated, the drive unit adjusts the rudder or wheel to correct any deviations. It keeps the boat on course despite wind, waves, or currents."

Eliza raised a hand to the view from the helm. "But clearly, the ship is driving itself. It had to be programmed to do that. Right?"

"Should we be concerned?" Beatrice asked, directing the question to Baxter.

He hesitated, lips pursed. "Any time a vessel does something it's not supposed to do, I'm concerned. However, once we get out of the harbor, the risk of a catastrophic collision is reduced, so there isn't anything you need to be concerned about in an immediate sense."

"I'll open up the control panel and see if I can find the problem," Mateo offered.

"I'd be happy to help," Eliza offered.

"I'll alert the harbor master," Baxter said, picking up the mic from its post over the console. "*Pleiades* to Malta Harbor Master, come in."

The radio crackled with static, but there was no response.

The yacht cleared the harbor, but continued on a course of its own choosing. Radio communication was down, as well as cell phone communications. The captain and his first mate were in a panic, though neither wanted to show it. Eliza helped as much as she could, but came to realize she was just in the way. Captain Baxter assured her they'd figure it out, and dismissed her.

Exhausted, Eliza was grateful for the assurance that they were in no immediate danger, and while nothing was under control, the best any of them could do was get some rest while they could. Having only picked at her dinner, she was feeling peckish. She could feel that her hair was wild, and she wanted to freshen up before she went to the galley to find something to eat. Esme was waiting for her.

"I figured it out," Esme said, shoving her sister into her own cabin, closing the door behind her. Eliza heard the *click* as it latched.

"What the hell, Ez—"

"This all started because you took the Compass from Solan's office," she insisted. "What happened to me on the dive ... that had to have something to do with it, too." Esme had already explained the bizarre events from her dive. After having seen the dive instructor when he boarded *The Pleiades*, Eliza had considered her sister might be smitten and not thinking rationally. That didn't explain the vision, but it did explain the anxiety and panic.

"Esme," Eliza caught her arm as Esme prattled on. Her younger sister froze and looked blankly at her. "Do you really think this has anything to do with the Compass?"

"I—" Esme started but hesitated. She shook her head and paced the foot of Eliza's bed. "We've had the opportunity to investigate two Artifacts so far. What did we learn about the Veil? About the Night Doctor's Blade?"

Eliza gave that a moment's thought. "The Veil was only part of the equation. It needed the Brooch in order to function."

"And the Artifact of Arkanos needed the trigger object to control each of its victims." Esme went on. "Where is the Compass now?"

"I put it in my suitcase," she said. She rose and retrieved her rolling carry-on that she'd tucked under the bed. She opened it, and took out the tee-shirt-wrapped object. She lay it on the bed and peeled away the cloth, careful not to touch it with her hand.

Esme moved beside her to study it. She took the hem of the shirt and rubbed at the markings, trying to clear the patina that obstructed what appeared to be writing. Eliza cocked her head, realizing Esme was on to something. "Does it look like there's a piece missing?" Esme asked as she worked, then backed away. She pointed to the prongs in the center.

Eliza took up the Compass, still using the shirt to hold it. She could feel the heft of it in her biceps. The brass was cold, ancient. Dust motes caught in a beam of the sconce on the wall as Esme turned it to shine on the Artifact. Eliza studied it, realizing the weight of what she'd done was a heavier burden. Elias had turned her into a thief, and she felt the wrongness of her actions in her core.

It didn't stop her from studying the intricate markings beneath the centuries-old patina. An inner dial surrounded a void where she'd already decided a piece was missing. The dial was engraved with a trident flanked by curling waves. Eliza noted four symbols that—at first—appeared to signify the four cardinal directions. Maybe not. Then her eye went to the letters Esme had revealed.

Μνημονεύετε Ἀτλαντίδα.

"How's your Greek?" Esme asked.

Eliza shook her head, but attempted to pronounce it. "Meem-o-ne-te Atlant-ee-da? Mimo-net Atlant-oh-ah?" She shrugged.

"I bet *Dr. Dreamboat* could translate it." Esme elbowed her with a chuckle that faded quickly. Eliza didn't flinch. Her fingers tightened around the cloth-covered Compass, even as she tried to let go.

It was subtle at first—a soft tremor through the sea that rocked the yacht. It felt like a heartbeat rather than a sound. Eliza felt the heat through her hands and dropped the Compass on the bed, staring at her trembling hands. She flexed her fingers to try and restore feeling in the tingling digits.

What in the hell just happened?

11

Spirit of the Sea

The Pleiades moved at a crawl, not so much propelled as *drawn*—four silent hours sliding over black water, Malta's light shrinking into the darkness behind them.

"I don't like this," Mateo said, scanning the gauges in the red light of the helm.

"Mateo, you haven't been aboard *The Pleiades* for long. I've worked for Solan Virell on-and-off for seven years." Captain Baxter's tone had no hint of alarm; rather, he seemed more curious about the bizarre mechanical anomaly than worried. "Having strange things happen is the norm around here. The boat steering itself is not the strangest thing I've seen, and we're paid *very* well not to ask questions. That's also why we all signed that oddly-worded NDA. No one is in danger at the moment, but when dawn shows its face, you can set out in the tender and go for help. Maybe you should grab a little sleep."

Mateo nodded, not satisfied with the non-explanation, but quite satisfied with the idea of going for help. At the rate they were going, they wouldn't be more than a dozen nautical miles away from Malta's mainland when dawn hit. They were only moving at three knots, certainly not ideal for dropping the small boat into the water, but do-able.

He stopped briefly in the crew mess to grab a bottle of water, and found Amalie huddled over a cup of tea.

"You want a cuppa?" she asked him.

He didn't really care for tea all that much, at least not in the middle of the night, but what he did want was her company. "Sure, thanks." He plopped down on the booth side of the small table.

She rose and poured him some of the steaming liquid, then set it in front of him and slid back into the booth beside him. "What did Bax say?"

"He didn't know what was causing it, but he's also shockingly unconcerned. At dawn, I'm taking the tender and heading back to the mainland to get some help."

"Very sensible," she sighed. Then she did something he didn't expect. She scooted closer and laid her head on his shoulder. He wondered if she could hear his thundering pulse. "I wish I could go with you."

He'd only known her for a few weeks, but every unencumbered moment filled his head with thoughts of her. The notion that she shared the feeling filled him with giddy joy. Happiness bubbled up within him, and he resisted the urge to laugh. Now wasn't a time for laughter. Instead he inclined his head to rest against her hair, the scent of her rosemary-mint shampoo tickling his nose. "I would love to have you with me, but maybe going for help is not a good first date."

He felt her body vibrate with a soft chuckle. "I guess you'll have to figure out some other outing for us, then."

Her affirmation boosted his confidence, and he snaked his arm around her, careful to bring his hand up to her bicep rather than presuming to hold her around the waist. He squeezed her gently and she leaned in closer, her breath brushing his neck.

"I will do that. Perhaps when this strange vacation is over, you would like to go for a walk with me through the Barratta Gardens. It is quite lovely there."

She raised her head to look at him, her eyes filled with surprise. "That would be ... marvelous."

"Is that alright? You seem taken aback."

"I'm just surprised. Usually the first thought anyone has for a first date is dinner."

"Oh, no." He shook his head. "You are a chef. That is far too risky. If we go out to eat, you must choose the place."

A slow smile spread across her cherubic face. "You've really thought this out."

He reflected her smile back at her. "I really, really have."

Far below the drifting yacht, the water rippled a living blue. Moonlight fractured into silver veins that shimmered and vanished in the depths. And from those depths, she awoke to the call of the Fathers.

She rose slowly, uncoiling from shadow, her movements effortless against the weight of the sea. Fins the color of a stormy sky caught the faint glow from above; her eyes reflected it back in twin shards of turquoise. She had worn many faces in her existence—goddess, spirit, monster—but the sea knew her by a different name. One it whispered only to the tides.

The Compass called to her. Even through leagues of water, she could feel its pulse—not sound, but memory, an echo from an age when the world had not yet decided what belonged above and below, what should be revealed, and what should be hidden away.

She circled *The Pleiades* once, feeling the rhythm of its engines like a human heartbeat gone awry. The mortals above were frightened. She could taste the sharpness of their fear in the current. They did not understand the thing they carried, or why it reached for the island's bones.

She smiled, or the sea's version of it, and answered the Fathers' call. With a flick of her tail, she grew smaller, sleeker, scales dimming to the silver grey and slate of a shark. She had promised not to interfere, of course. But promises, like the tides, were meant to shift, after all.

As the yacht followed the Compass's pull, she glided along behind, curious if the two turtle doves who so vexed the Fathers would find what had been hidden for so long.

Dawn broke over a motionless sea. The island of Filfla rose ahead of them—an iron-grey slab of rock streaked with salt and shadow, uninhabited since anyone could remember. No harbor, no trees, only the whisper of surf against broken cliffs.

Without human command, *The Pleiades* slowed and dropped her anchor. The chains rattled and fell silent. In Eliza's cabin, the feeling of a sigh, though not the sound of one, woke her. She threw on an ecru cotton caftan and made her way to the salon. She spotted Niko standing along the transom with his hands on his hips. It occurred to her that they hadn't seen him during the late-night alarm. She slid open the glass door and he turned, startled.

"Good morning," she greeted him. The tangerines and violets of sunrise were just beginning to bleed into the sky.

"Um, yes, good morning. You'll forgive me, I hope, if I'm a bit discombobulated. This is not the sight I expected to see when I stepped out on deck today."

She thought fast. It was probably best if she didn't reveal that *The Pleiades* had had a mind of her own during the night. Niko was a dive instructor, not an Aegis Agent. "It seems the crew decided to take us to another lovely location last night."

"Yes, well, they've brought us to a restricted area. Filfla," he groused, pointing to the islet off the stern, "is a protected nature reserve, and boats aren't permitted within a nautical mile. It looks to me like we're a bit closer than that." His jaw was set in consternation.

"Oh, my. I'm sure there's some misunderstanding ..." she began, knowing she shouldn't say much. No one had thought to get their stories straight for his benefit in all the hullabaloo the night before. "I'll go up to the bridge and ask." She made a hasty retreat.

She could feel Niko's eyes on her back as she made her escape. The water rippled slightly, and a blue shark slipped beneath the hull, silent as thought.

Eliza found Bax at the helm, a similarly bothered look on his face. "I take it from your expression that you know we shouldn't be here."

Bax nodded. "We're closer than we should be, which will get us slapped with a citation if some tourist boat comes along and sees us, but as long as we don't try to go ashore, we won't get into quite as much trouble. Apparently whatever brought us here doesn't care much about environmental regulations."

"What's the plan? Niko's already in a lather about it, and we never even discussed what to tell him."

"One more problem on my list. Best thing we can do is claim engine failure, probably. We were making a night passage and ran into trouble. Mateo is taking the tender back to the mainland for help."

"That sounds plausible enough." Eliza nodded her approval.

"It will have to do. Could you please spread the word on that? I've learned not to ask a lot of questions on this boat, but Niko isn't part of our crew, and he hasn't signed any NDAs. We need to keep this need-to-know."

"Understood," she agreed. She swung quickly back by the cockpit where Niko was still seething, then headed below deck to make sure everyone else knew what to say.

By the time she'd dressed and come back to the salon, Simon and Mateo had joined Niko at the stern. She noted that he didn't look nearly as annoyed as he had before, and she took that as a good sign.

"... some sort of bizarre interference," Mateo was saying. "Captain Baxter is lowering the tender into the water, and I'm going to grab a few supplies and see if I can't get a tug to tow us back to a nearby marina." The scraping sound of the winch verified Mateo's story, and Eliza saw the small vessel being lowered into the water out one of the side windows.

"How long do you think that will take?" Niko asked.

"Maybe two or three hours, tops. Depends on how fast a tug can be available. It's not too far to the marina, I don't think." Mateo made his way to the side deck and tied the tender off on to a low cleat. Then he returned and reached for the door to the salon. "I need to get a few supplies to take with me."

"Thank you for doing this," Simon smiled, clapping him on the shoulder. Through the open doorway he spotted Eliza nibbling a cranberry-orange scone from the tray Amalie had left on the coffee table. "Oh, good morning, my dear!" He and Niko followed Mateo inside, perching on the settee near the tray of pastries.

Beneath the yacht, a shadow curled upward, sleek and playful. A flash of silver teeth, the flick of a tail—one quick slice through the mooring line. The tender drifted free, caught by a mild current, then tugged along by something unseen toward Filfla's stony cliffs.

When Mateo returned with his supplies in his backpack and Amalie by his side, the tender was already a speck in the distance. He hollered up to the bridge, and Bax clambered down the stairs to see what the problem might be. He found Mateo with the remnants of the line in his hand.

"What the—did the line snap?"

Mateo held up the remaining end, examining the clean edges. "It didn't snap, sir. It was cut."

The Pleiades floated motionless, the swell barely lifting her hull. No one spoke for a long while, and Esme and Beatrice had joined them in their silence. Even the usual sounds of the sea had gone strangely quiet as if the world were waiting for something to happen.

Finally, Captain Baxter stood up and stared out the large starboard window. "Whatever this is, it isn't weather and it isn't current. I'm going to try the sat phone again." He half-walked, half stomped off toward the helm.

Eliza stood and muttered something about going to her cabin, and Esme followed behind her. The others stood and stared toward the island. The air felt charged, thick with salt and static. Even the gulls that had followed them from Malta were gone. Only the mirror sea and the stone face of Filfla remained.

Below deck, in Eliza's cabin, the Compass pulsed faintly through the tee shirt she'd wrapped it in. Its metal throbbed like a heartbeat trying to sync with another far away. Eliza had a sense that the pulses rippled out like sonar in the depths around the hull.

"It's calling," Esme said, materializing at Eliza's door. "It wants us to listen."

"When we both touched it before, it took control of the ship. Are you saying we should do it again?" Eliza was skeptical.

"I think we have to if we want to know why it brought us here."

Reluctantly, Eliza let the shirt fall away and felt the bronze warm against her skin. She looked up at Esme and nodded once, not trusting her voice to agree to this harebrained scheme. Esme raised her own hands until the Compass was cradled between them.

The Artifact answered with a single bright pulse, bright enough to reflect off the portholes beside Eliza's bed. Then, from somewhere beneath the hull, a low resonant sound rose, somewhere between a sigh and a note of music. It vibrated through the boat, through bone and breath, until Eliza thought she could just make out words hidden inside it, fragments of a language older than water.

Esme heard it, too, but her eyes had gone milky and her lips were forming silent words as the Compass whispered to her. *She was swimming, swimming, and part of her knew exactly where she was. She could see and feel the sun's rays passing through the sea's surface as her fins undulated her body and propelled her through the water.*

She could see the rocks, submerged deeply now under the tides, the island a maze of fissures and hollows. In one of those hollows, the sunlight glinted off of something red—a flicker of color gone as quickly as it appeared.

She blinked and she was back in Eliza's cabin, her sister patiently keeping still until the vision had run its course.

"It's waiting." Esme's voice came out in a harsh whisper.

"For what?" asked Eliza.

Esme's eyes had cleared, but her mind was still focused on the forbidden island. "For me."

12

Forbidden Waters

"No. Absolutely not." Simon put his foot down. Eliza and Beatrice stood in solidarity behind him. Esme had already had this argument with her sister, the captain and her dive instructor. It didn't stop her from donning her dive suit, and sitting on the transom while she adjusted the straps on her BCD.

Niko appeared from below deck with his equipment in hand. He wore a pair of speedos and a T-shirt but the expression on his face was sober. "The first rule of diving is never dive alone."

It was a rule she was prepared to break. "I have to do this, but I won't ask you to risk your professional certifications on it."

"I won't let you go alone." Niko stated flatly, already donning his dive suit and dive gear. "I must advise you though, it's illegal, immoral, and just plain foolhardy, but I am responsible for your safety and if you are resolute in going, I'm going with you. Certifications be damned."

Her family wasn't so acquiescent.

"Esme, you can't go down there," Beatrice said only because Esme appeared to be ignoring her father. "Are you not listening? Everyone on this yacht is telling you not to go. You are inexperienced and being ruinous. And you're not just putting yourself in danger, you're putting Niko in danger, too."

That made Esme hesitate.

Niko sat on the transom beside her, looking like a whipped dog who was obeying his master. She could tell he didn't want to go, but he wouldn't let her go alone. Just as she was about to capitulate simply for his sake, something struck the side of the vessel hard enough that it pitched and yawed, upending Esme.

One minute she was sitting beside Niko, the next, she plunged into the water on her back, one fin on, the other still in her hand. She surfaced, pulling on her mask, purging water from it. But something wasn't right. Her buoyancy control device wasn't working and she could feel herself being pulled down. With one fin, she wasn't strong enough to fight it. She barely had a chance to cry out before she submerged into the briny deep.

"Esme!" Beatrice called out after her. Even Eliza raced to the rail to look for her sister, seeing the shadow disappearing as she sank.

"I'll get her." Niko raced to don his equipment, gave it a quick double check, then pitched himself over backwards.

Rhea gazed through the binoculars, watching as the youngest Wren girl went overboard. "Doesn't she know these are restricted waters?"

"Clearly, she doesn't care," Charmaine was already on her second martini. She was put out by the whole affair. She was only here to keep an eye on the Artifact, not play secret babysitter to the Wrens on holiday. Captain Baxter had been a good and reliable employee but now she had questions, questions she would get answers to.

Maybe Baxter had the right idea. Who needed a man like Solan Virell when you had control of assets like *The Pleiades*? He could do whatever he wanted and the Grand Aegis would never know unless someone told him. She could do the same. She *should* do the same. Clearly, Solan would never see her as anything more than a secretary. That could not be allowed to stand. Once she figured out what Baxter and the Wrens were up to, she would show him. She'd show them all!

Wait. A thought struck her like a rogue wave. *Did they know? How could they?* Only three people knew there was an Artifact on Solan's ship. Solan knew it. Elias knew it. She knew it. It had been her idea, actually, though she didn't tell Elias that. Would he have even remembered after all these years?

Solan had always loved the sea, and he once raced sailboats competitively. However, his last sailboat was lost in a vicious storm, and Solan nearly went down with it. A fellow sailor abandoned the race and came to his rescue, plucking him from the roiling seas at the last possible minute.

It'd taken him a long time before he wanted to get another boat, but decided his days racing on a monohull sailboat were over, and catamarans had never appealed to him. Charmaine had come with him to shop for a new vessel, and had actually been the one that suggested a better security net than anything he could ever imagine.

Deep within the Vaults under St. Paul's Cathedral, the Order secured Artifacts away from the Obsidian Covenant, including a Compass that once crossed paths with the Manifest. Little did the Order know what they really had. Randall thought he knew the truth, but Charmaine had other sources.

Family legend had it that this was the original Compass used by her ancestor Timaeus himself, as he fled Atlantis the night the island was claimed by the sea. Charmaine needed it somewhere she could access it if the time ever came, and she'd every intention of removing it from his yacht if there were ever a chance of needing to use it herself. She couldn't reach it in the Vaults, but Solan, as the Grand Aegis, could.

"It's not like you're stealing it from the Order," she'd suggested to him when the topic came up. "You're just reallocating it to a security detail. The legend says no ship can sink when the Compass is on board. Timaeus himself should have drowned in the escape from Atlantis, but he made it to Kemet. The Compass protected him. It will protect you, too."

Solan was a sucker.

A week before *The Pleiades* was re-christened, he went into the Vaults himself and took the Compass from the crate where it was stored. He replaced it with a cheap replica he commissioned from a sketch, and sealed the crate back up. Had the bloody Wren girls found it? Had they figured out how to use it? Did they know what the Compass led to?

"She won't be down there long," Rhea drew Charmaine from her thoughts. She came over to stand beside her sister.

"Why do you say that?"

Rhea handed over the binoculars and pointed towards the waters. Charmaine adjusted the focus looking for what might compel the Wren girl out of the sea. A dark fin rose, circling the boat. Then, another. "Sharks?" Charmaine asked.

"Most likely blue sharks, or possibly black tips or hammerheads," Rhea said.

"Are there white sharks in the Mediterranean?" Corrine asked, glancing up from her book.

"Rarely," Charmaine said, scanning *The Pleiades,* and those aboard it. Simon Wren stood with his arms crossed, though his expression was difficult to make out, even with the binoculars, but if she had to wager a guess, he looked angry. Surely he must know what his daughters were up to, maybe he just didn't like it.

Niko saw the shark just before it made a whipping turn towards Esme. His pupil was on her back, being dragged deeper. Bubbles rising from her mask told him she had at least gotten the regulator valve turned on before she'd fallen overboard. He usually carried a blade strapped to his leg whenever he was in the water, but in his haste, he hadn't put it on. Even if he could get to her in time, he had no way to defend her from the creature other than his own brute strength.

To his surprise, the shark turned away before it reached the girl, and now it had its beady eyes fixed on him. The creature circled silently, blocking him from reaching Esme, even as he dumped air from his buoyancy control so he could descend with ease. "Esme, can you hear me?" he said through the mic in his mask.

"Niko," a tentative response came a beat later.

"You're descending too fast," he noted. "Adjust your BCD."

"I'm trying," she answered, panic heavy in her voice.

"Stay calm. There's a regulator switch at your left shoulder. Find it?"

He could see her reach for it, patting her upper arm, and noted when her hand steadied. "Got it."

"Hit the inflate button." He spoke calmly to assure her. "Press the button down."

"It's not working," she cried out. "What do I do?"

"It's okay, Esme. There's a manual override. Take a deep breath. I got you." He didn't, but she didn't need to know that. The shark seemed to be sizing him up, but he was more concerned for Esme than himself at that moment. "There's a pullcord at your hip. It'll release CO_2 from a cartridge in the BCD unit."

Esme found the ripcord and pulled it. Niko could hear the hiss of the canister filling the BCD, and observed her descent slow, as her body righted in the water. "There you go. How're your ears?"

"Not good," she answered. "I don't know how to do the Valsalva maneuver with this mask."

"You'll have to do the Frenzel maneuver." The shark had moved away, but he could see other shadows in the distance, and knew there was more than one to worry about. "Close your mouth and use your tongue and throat muscles to push air into the Eustachian tubes. Can you do that?"

"Got it," Esme said. "That's better."

"We need to get back up to the boat," Niko said, just as he reached out for Esme's hand. Their fingers touched as she was suddenly yanked downward. Niko kicked hard and tried again, this time catching the back of her BCD. The force that drew her down pulled him down, too.

"What the—"

"It's not my BCD," Esme said. "I can't control this."

"I won't leave you alone down here." Niko tried adjusting his own device, pulling on his emergency rip cord, but it didn't seem to do any good. "It's important not to panic, Esme. I don't think this rate of descent is going to put either of us at risk, but we aren't supposed to be here, and you're not qualified to dive at these depths."

"It doesn't feel like I have much of a choice," she responded. "I've felt the pull even when I was on *The Pleiades*. There's something down here I have to find."

Niko had never done work for the Aegis Order before, but he knew better than to ask questions. While he wasn't one of them, he knew they did work that no military or government agency could do. "Let's focus on managing the situation ..." he instructed. "You have to tell me if you begin to feel any ill effects from the pressure. Your body isn't accustomed to this."

"I'm okay," she assured him, but the tone of her voice suggested otherwise.

The water darkened as they descended. The force that moved them finally leveled off roughly ten metres from the bottom, according to Niko's dive computer. Their movement became more vertical and Niko released his grip, realizing he was now being drawn down, too. He activated the torch on his sleeve and directed it at the rocks that appeared around them, the walls of a cave enveloping them.

"I guess I'm not qualified for cave diving either?" Esme's tentative question found him as he studied the water reflecting his light against the sheer stone walls. A carnelian glow filled the space in the distance.

"Not even close," he said. "Cave diving is only for advanced divers."

"But you are? Right?"

"I am," he said. "The most important thing is not to get disoriented, or too close to the cave walls. You could get snagged or trapped in the cave."

Esme's hand snaked into his. "I'm scared," she admitted.

"You should be cautious, but not scared. I won't let anything happen to you." She turned and met his gaze, his blue eyes illuminated by the dim light in his mask.

"Just don't let me out of your sight," she said. "I won't panic."

The force that compelled them forward began to lift them in the water. Esme raised her eyes, and she realized the glow came from above. Water shimmered in bright columns that swirled on waves as they broke the surface, the void around them, tinged in a pulsing, throbbing red glow.

"Keep your mask on," Niko said. "We don't know if there's enough oxygen in this cavern."

Esme nodded, as she moved to a place where the water grew shallow and a sandy beach provided dry land. She took off her fins, following Niko's lead.

There was a tunnel leading away from the water, where the glow seemed to beckon Esme. There was a tunnel leading away from the water, where the glow seemed to beckon Esme. The coral walls had been worn smooth by the repeated beating of the tides as they cycled through the centuries. The swirl of greys and pinks reminded Esme of the human brain, but hers was stuck on the thought, *why does it always have to be tunnels?*

Niko caught her hand again. She realized her rate of breathing had increased, and she was sucking down air too fast. With his hand to calm her, she allowed her breathing to slow, and they moved together, cautiously.

Esme could hear her pulse throbbing in her temples, and she realized the thrum ahead matched the tempo of her calming heart. The cavern began to narrow, but still remained passable, the sand damp beneath their bare feet told her the tide would rise and flood the chamber, though how long until high tide was beyond her ken.

"What is that?" Niko's voice sounded in her earpiece.

Esme straightened as they neared what appeared to be a room with man-made stairs that led to what looked like an altar. A statue rose behind it, and Esme recognized it as Calypso, a minor goddess in Greek mythology, daughter of Atlas. The glowing heartbeat hung around the statue's neck. Niko scanned the idol with his flashlight, pausing on what appeared to be an intricately cut ruby set in the shell of a nautilus. His light created a disco-ball effect and beams of red light fanned out to touch every corner of the void.

"What does that say?" Esme pointed to ancient letters carved into the arch above the statue. Niko shined his light on it. "Is that Greek?"

"It is," he said, reading it. "Είμαι το κύμα που θυμάται."

"Well, it's all Greek to me. Can you translate that?"

"Yes, of course. It's my native language. It says *I am the tide that remembers*. That's the first line." He moved his light. "Κρύβω μόνο ό,τι δεν είναι ακόμη έτοιμο να βρεθεί. *I conceal only what is not yet ready to be found.*"

Wow, pretty and smart. No wonder he captivated her interest.

She moved beneath the statue, trying to get a better look at the stone that hung from a golden chain around the statue's neck. Esme reached for it, but it was too far above her, even if she stood on her tippy toes.

The cavern around them began to tremble, and the statue stirred, awakened as if by forces not of their world. "Εσύ που φέρεις την τραυματισμένη καρδιά της θάλασσας... το κύμα σε θυμάται." Her voice came from deep within the marble body, deep and commanding.

Niko quickly translated, "*You who bear the broken heart of the sea ... the tide remembers you.*"

Esme swallowed hard. "Me?"

The nymph's statue continued, as Niko translated her words like a whisper in Esme's ear.

"The Compass calls, the stone still weeps,
For what was lost beneath the deeps.
Four gates await the daring few,
Beyond the seas the mortals view,
And when all else is cast away,
The Heart must choose the price to pay."

Esme cast a cautionary gaze back at Niko. He stood transfixed as if he were caught in one of her visions. His blue eyes had gone white, and he spoke the words in the language Esme knew, as if they were a magic spell.

"Follow the silver dolphins wake,
To where the sky and sea converge to break,
There lies the Gate, hidden still,

The portal bows to no man's will.

But beware, child of air and flame,"

Still standing beneath the statue, Esme heard the clink of metal as the clasp of the necklace broke or came undone. She had but a second to react. She caught the stone and stumbled back, set off balance by the air tank between her shoulders. Niko, still caught in the vision, launched forward and caught her. The goddess's message continued.

"Three shadows bear a hidden name

They guard the path, they guard the key

Atlantis sleeps for none but thee."

13

Common Ground

"What do you mean you can't get a signal?" Phillip looked in disbelief at the empty slip where *The Pleiades* had been the night before. "They were supposed to be in Malta for three more days."

"How can I be more clear?" Elias crossed his arms over his chest.

"Maybe they just left early for a daytrip somewhere ..." Phillip rationalized. The notion sounded unlikely, even to his own ears. Eliza would have mentioned it if they were leaving port.

Elias gave him a hard look. "The harbourmaster said they didn't notify the marina office about a departure. Nor is their transponder transmitting their location. The last ping had them heading south."

The older man was perplexed. "And you aren't getting a GPS signal from Eliza's phone?" He opened his own phone and navigated to the *recent calls* tab.

"Do you need me to say it more slowly?"

Phillip set his jaw and hit the call button on Eliza's number, only to get a recording that the cellular customer in question was outside the service area. He resisted the urge to rise to Elias's bait. They'd been traveling together for three days, following *The Pleiades's* movements from land, and it had been an uncomfortable truce, to say the least. They stared at each other, a mutual challenge thick in the air. Phillip broke first. "You still think Charmaine is behind it."

"I *know* she is."

"You also *knew* your parents were lying to you," Phillip retorted, and immediately regretted it.

Elias narrowed his eyes. "You're going to bring that up *now*?"

"You dug it up when you disappeared and let everyone think you died," Phillip said. "People talk, Elias. You must know that. The rumor was ancient even when we trained together. I thought you'd make peace with it, even when that legacy asshat brought it up when you beat his marksmanship score on the training course."

"Peace?" Elias laughed bitterly. "You mean accept that half the Order thought I was Niall Roth's bastard?"

Phillip didn't answer. The angle of the sunlight picked out the scar along Elias's chin that he hadn't had back then.

"I never cared about the gossip," Phillip said finally. "You were the best in our cohort, and everyone knew it. But you left your family to bury an empty coffin. You let *her* grieve you."

"Don't talk to me about why I left," Elias snapped. "My father refused the test. Mother swore she couldn't remember what happened on that mission with Niall. Everytime I looked at them after that, all I saw was the question they wouldn't answer. Maybe you can live with that kind of lie. I couldn't. I was sick of the corruption and betrayal. Solan was *and is* compromised, and for all I know, my parents are, too."

"You think I've had an easy time with truth?" Phillip's voice was low, steady. "You know as well as I do that service to the Order sometimes means taking things on faith. You're the one who jumps to conclusions about answers you don't have."

Elias stared at the thin silver line of horizon. "Maybe that's all I'm good for—asking the wrong questions."

"There's a difference between questioning authority and subverting it," Phillip pointed out. "But we're both good at surviving things we shouldn't, apparently. Let's start there."

Elias nodded at the weak attempt at an olive branch. "Here's what we know: Charmaine and two other women snuck into the marina at Salerno and boarded a boat called *Naxos* in the middle of the night. They started following *The Pleiades* when it departed the next day and presumably have been following ever since."

"If Solan had sent Charmaine, it wouldn't have been so secretive," Phillip allowed. "So why didn't you mention it to Eliza when you texted her?"

"I didn't want to *jump to conclusions,*" Elias answered with just a touch of acid.

"But you're not suspicious enough that you want me to alert Solan?"

"I told you, Solan can't be trusted either. Are you starting to see why I left the Order?"

Phillip chose not to honour that with a reply. "And you're sure Eliza wouldn't have just turned off her GPS once she realized you were tracking her?"

"It was a gamble," Elias admitted. "But Eliza won't do anything to purposely make herself less safe."

Phillip had to confess that this was likely true. "So we should assume something is interfering with the signals from *The Pleiades.* And we should assume that, whatever it is, your family may have been Shanghaied against their will."

"We'll need a boat," Elias said.

"Then we'll find one."

The grotto seemed darker than when they first arrived. So did Niko. His expression was blank, confused, disoriented. And that was a problem because *he* was the experienced cave diver.

Esme hung the Ruby pendant around her own neck and zipped it up into her wetsuit. "Niko." She nudged him, but he barely seemed aware of her. "Niko! Come back from wherever you are! We need to get out of here and back to the boat while we still have air in the tanks." She shook his shoulder and he blinked at her, still dazed.

"Back to the boat," he repeated.

"Yes, we—" Before she could finish her sentence, he turned away and ambled toward the water's edge. Something in his movement reminded her of Romania—of Alban. She felt a pang of grief, but swallowed it down as Niko stepped off the edge of the rocks and into the water. Esme followed, hoping he would automatically swim his way out and she could trail behind him. If he ended up needing assistance or rescue in a cave, she wasn't sure what she would do.

He was swimming slowly, backtracking the path that had brought them to the hidden grotto. The light was weak here and Esme switched on the LED light strip inside her mask. Though the scarlet glow the Ruby radiated was no longer illuminating the darkness, Esme could feel the warmth and the pulse of it against her skin.

Esme and Niko kicked back toward the narrow tunnel (why were there *always* tunnels?) that led back into the open water. The current pressed against them, stronger now, as if reluctant to let them go. She drew alongside Niko and switched on his LED as well before he entered the twisting rock corridor.

The cave seemed to have changed. Shadows pooled in the crevices where she thought she had seen smooth limestone only moments before. Something shimmered deep within the fissures—a flicker of gold-green, gone as soon as the lights touched it. Esme froze. A dark shape slid from one crack to another, its movement sinuous and silent.

Moray eels.

Three, maybe four of them, their long bodies winding through the stone like living ropes. Their eyes, glassy and pale, caught the light, and their jaws opened and closed in a slow rhythm. Niko's light lingered on one of them too long—it lashed out, striking inches from his fingers. Esme jerked him back, and together they struck the wall. The sound echoed, magnified in the closed space as it reverberated through the water.

Esme held her breath. The eels turned toward the sound and vibrations, their bodies weaving together in an uneasy dance. She felt the Ruby pulse once against her chest, reassuring and warm. The nearest eel paused, its mouth half-open, then slowly withdrew into the darkness as if reconsidering.

We're protected. The thought came to her as a certainty. She edged ahead of Niko and took his hand, drawing him forward carefully and slowly. The eels followed the movement for a moment, then vanished deeper into the stone, leaving the water strangely clear again.

As they swam past the last bend, a faint but glowing shimmer passed across Esme's skin, like sunlight through stained glass. For a heartbeat, she thought she saw the outline of a woman in the rippling light, smiling faintly and giving Esme a playful wink before fading into the current.

Then the tunnel widened. The sea beyond was open and blue. Esme kicked hard and Niko followed suit, breaking the surface in a surge of foam and gasping against the bright glare of daylight.

The sea had gone unnaturally still again. *The Pleiades* had ridden the current to the edge of the restricted zone before the water had gone glassy-smooth, and everyone's relief was palpable when they spotted Esme and Niko swimming back. They were a little less relieved when they saw Niko's expression. Mateo stepped in, citing some experience as a military medic, and guided the dive instructor down to the crew quarters.

Niko's color had returned by the time Mateo got him below, but his eyes were still distant, unfocused, glazed. Esme followed close behind as Mateo checked his pulse, pupils, and responses.

"Vitals are good. Shock, probably. Maybe mild hypoxia? He's rattled, but he'll come around," Mateo said, pressing a bottle of water into Niko's hands.

Niko blinked at Esme, brow furrowing as recognition began to return. "You ... you found something down there, didn't you?"

"Just moray eels and bad decisions."

His lips twitched in a faint, confused grin. "Thought so."

Mateo gave her a quick look—the kind that said he knew there was more to the story but also that he wasn't going to pry. "He'll be fine. Let him rest. You should get warm and hydrated, too."

She nodded, her heart pounding, the weight and warmth of the Ruby pressing against her chest beneath her wetsuit.

When the decks had quieted down and the crew returned to their duties, Esme climbed the steps to the salon. The yacht felt too large, too silent—almost like the sea itself was listening.

She found her family assembled in the salon, and their concerned faces gave her clarity about what must be done. "Could we reassemble downstairs in your stateroom?" She nodded toward her parents, but then turned on her heel so they wouldn't have the chance to ask why. After a faint mumble of voices, she heard footsteps following her.

Within minutes, the family had gathered: Simon by the porthole, Beatrice sitting on the edge of the bed, and Eliza standing by her sister, her arms folded tightly across her chest. Esme closed the door before she spoke.

"We need to talk. All of us."

Beatrice frowned. "Esme, is this about your dive?"

"It's about everything. About what's happening to this ship."

Eliza's expression tightened, but she nodded. "She's right. There's something you need to know." She slipped out of the cabin and returned a moment later, her arms carrying a bundle wrapped in a tee shirt. The room fell silent as she unwrapped the Compass. Its brass casing caught the light, the empty space at the center dark and hollow.

"Elias told me about it," she muttered. "He said Solan was keeping it hidden, using it for himself. I didn't believe him at first, but I ... broke into Solan's cabin. It was there, as Elias said it would be."

Simon blanched. "You what?"

Beatrice pressed a hand to her mouth. "Eliza—"

"You think I wanted to do this?" Eliza snapped, then softened. "I had to see for myself."

Simon rubbed his hand over his jaw. "Solan may be many things, but I've never known him to risk people's lives for greed. There has to be another explanation."

"Like what? He's been secreting off at least one Artifact, probably more. And now that we found it, *The Pleiades* has a mind of its own. What explanation fits that?"

Beatrice looked between her daughters, torn. "Solan has protected the Order for decades. He's been a friend to this family since before you were born."

"Friends don't hide relics of unknown power," Eliza said.

Simon's voice was low. "Maybe he didn't know what it was. Maybe he thought it was just an antique—" The excuse sounded weak, even to him.

"He should have known," Esme answered. "I think I might have an idea, and I'm not as powerful as he is."

She reached into her pocket and pulled out the Ruby Nautilus. The gem caught the lamplight, scattering prisms of red light across the walls. The stone pulsed, faintly, but definitely.

"This was in a grotto below Filfla," she said. "Guarded. Hidden. And it fits in the center."

She held it near the Compass and the metal seemed to hum in response, a low resonant vibration.

The family stared at it, transfixed and uneasy.

"Don't," Beatrice warned. "Don't join them. We know what the Compass can do already."

Esme looked down at the Ruby, the faint reflection of her own eyes burning in its facets. "But if I'm right, the Compass isn't what's controlling the ship anymore."

"Then what is?" Simon asked.

Esme met Eliza's surprised gaze. "A goddess with her own agenda."

14

Trust and Trespass

The Wren girl took her father's hand as he hoisted her onto the boat. The Captain stood by to steady her. Charmaine recognized Baxter by the cut of his jacket. The second diver didn't come up so easily. Something was wrong. Members of the crew gathered around him. The first mate, Mateo Laskaris, helped him down to the crew quarters and out of sight.

Simon Wren looked angry. His wife looked concerned. The Wren girl looked like she was hiding something, even as her older sister grabbed her and held onto her in a hug that lasted far too long for Charmaine's comfort. She didn't feel like that about either of her sisters. The Andrews family weren't *huggers*. But that's how Charmaine liked it. They rarely saw each other, but when Charmaine got suspicious about Solan letting the Wrens use his yacht—knowing what was onboard—she felt the need to call in her sisters. The three of them worked well together. Charmaine was the brains, Rhea the brawn, and Corrine was just bold enough to get them in and out of tight situations.

"We have to get on that boat," Charmaine muttered to herself as she lowered her binoculars.

Corrine quipped,"What are we gonna do? Sneak over there in the middle of the night and just waltz aboard?"

"I need in Solan's office," Charmaine said. "All the answers I need are there."

"I know a high ranking official in the Italian Coast Guard," Rhea offered. "She could have their ship boarded and any absconded Artifacts seized."

"No," Charmaine answered. "We can't involve anyone, least of all a government official. This is something we'll have to take care of ourselves."

"Char, we *can't* just sneak over there in the middle of the night," Corrine stated flatly. Her tone might have been flippant when she suggested it, but now she was resolute in her statement.

"I've got a couple of hours to come up with a plan." Charmaine stowed her binoculars and rose, snatching her martini glass off the table.

Phillip nearly leapt out of his skin when his phone pinged in his shirt pocket. His tracking app blinked as he opened the program and saw Eliza's phone was now transmitting her location. It flickered and he panicked, taking a screenshot just before it flashed and faded, the dot no longer visible.

"What is it?" Elias must have seen the look on his face.

"For a moment, I had a ping from Eliza's phone," he said. There was no point in hiding it. He turned the wheel in the direction her transponder had indicated, but he didn't mention he'd gotten a screen shot of the app before he lost her signal.

"Where was she?" Elias asked.

Phillip put his finger on the screen where the blip had been, then zoomed in for more detail on the map.

"Filfla? No. That can't be right. That ... that's a restricted area," Elias protested.

"I hope I'm wrong," Philip said. "That's the most forbidden island in the Mediterranean."

"And for good reason," Elias agreed, having to raise his voice as Phillip gunned the engines of their small craft. "The Royal Navy used Filfla island for bombing practice for decades. There are hundreds of unexploded ordinances scattered on the islands, and even getting within a nautical mile of that place can get you locked up, or at the least, heavily fined."

"It's not like your sister to go somewhere she's not supposed to," Phillip stated. "If she's at Filfla Island, it may be against her will."

"Are you thinking ... pirates?"

"It happens," Phillip said. "Even in these modern times, pirates see a yacht like *The Pleiades* as a cash cow. The coast of Africa is a hot bed for pirates and human trafficking. It puts everyone on that ship at risk."

"I can hardly see my father being—"

"Nowadays, human trafficking is more about politics and power—or money. Your family would make a handsome ransom if they knew who to demand money from."

"And what would happen if someone didn't pay?" Elias's expression suggested he was already putting the pieces together. Neither of them liked the possibilities.

"Let's just worry about finding them before someone else does," Phillip swallowed hard, giving the throttle a bit more juice.

The small sea going craft had seen better days. The sound of the hull hitting the driving waves echoed through the soles of Phillip's shoes, and he wished he'd come to Italy better prepared for a sea cruise. He'd intended to visit Eliza just long enough to make a brief appearance, then return to his work at Pompeii. He hadn't expected to run into a ghost.

There had been a time when he considered Elias Wren a friend. They'd been in the same cohort of new recruits when he joined Aegis. Of course, Phillip was older than the other trainees. He'd already graduated *Summa Cum Laude* from the University of Chicago with a dual bachelor's degree in linguistics and pre-med, a masters in both philosophy and history and completed his studies at Johns Hopkins University School of Medicine and Department of Anthropology, obtaining a dual PhD/MD. That made him highly sought after by the Order.

Elias was still a cocky and brash young man with a legacy to protect. The Wren family name gave him some clout. It didn't hurt that he was considered the golden boy of their unit. Elias was smarter, stronger, and more agile. Of course, Phillip had more extensive education, but that could only get one so far in a world where training was as equally valuable. Still, Elias could out shoot, out fight, out run Phillip, who didn't learn he had an astigmatism until he'd gone in for a medical evaluation after he and Elias sparred in hand-to-hand combat and Elias had sucker punched him in the side of the head. The blow knocked him out cold, and got Elias written up for excessive force against a classmate.

"I never held it against you," Phillip said, out of the blue.

"It sure felt like it," Elias must have been thinking the same thing. "I was the one that got transferred to a lower cohort."

"I didn't ask the Order to do that," Phillip said. "I let my guard down and you took advantage of it. You did what I might have done had the roles been reversed."

"I hated Solan for that," Elias snorted. "It wasn't fair."

"No. It wasn't."

"I saw you kiss my sister."

"Your sister and I have become quite ... close."

"Oh, yeah?" Elias balled his fists, a move that did not go unnoticed as Phillip piloted the craft. "How close?"

"I've kissed her a couple of times," Phillip stated. "Not that it's any of your affair."

"Do you love her?" Elias demanded.

Phillip pursed his lips and drew in a deep breath of the gusting sea air through his nose. His head was already nodding in the affirmative before he could get the words out. "I do."

"If you hurt her, I'll knock you out again. I've got nothing left to lose."

Elias's words were firm, and left no doubt in Phillip's mind that he meant it. "That's the last thing I want to do. Eliza keeps her heart locked away. She doesn't share it easily, and it's evident that it's been hurt before. I think part of that has to do with what you did."

Elias snapped, "What I did is none of *your* business."

"Just like my relationship with Eliza is none of *your* business."

Eliza sat on the forward deck as the sun set over the Mediterranean Sea, a half-empty glass of lemon squash on the table in front of her. The shadows of the day played on the rock that was Filfla. The Dingli Cliffs reminded her of Dover as the island jutted sixty metres above the dark blue waters. A smaller island, Filfoletta, looked like a pebble next to its much larger sister. Seabirds hovered over the islands, including British storm petrels and yellow-legged gulls. She could hear their haunting cries on the wind.

These birds were one of the many reasons these waters were restricted. Rare species of wild leeks, lizards, and snails were all endemic to the island.

She'd been terrified when Esme had gone overboard so unexpectedly. The entire time she and Niko were gone, Eliza's anxiety had spun out of control. She tried texting Phillip, but whatever had blocked the ship's communication systems had taken out cell service, too. Her phone repeatedly gave her a "*Message Delivery: Failed*" response, and she'd finally given up trying and deleted the message.

It occurred to her, as she sat scanning the horizon, that no one had ever made Eliza feel more safe than Phillip. Not even Esme, though the comfort of her sister's presence was something that gave her peace. Peace and safety were two different things. *Or were they?*

She needed both, especially for those times when her job offered neither. The time she spent working with Phillip Thorpe in Romania made her realize that.

Aegis normally assigned Agents in partners, but she wondered if an exception could be made. Phillip, Esme, and Eliza could be a force to be reckoned with if they were given a chance to work as a trio. *Would Solan even allow that?*

Solan. The very thought of him made her hair stand on end, despite the warm, humid evening that faded quickly into night. If Solan truly was using Artifacts for his own personal gain, there had to be some version of checks and balances to protect the Order, right? Her parents knew now about the Compass, and Esme had found its missing piece. Why would Solan keep the Compass on his yacht? If she had the internet, she could look it up in the Aegis Database. Or better yet, she could call Randall. Surely he'd know something about it. Right?

"Penny for your thoughts." Esme came up and found her lost in thought. Eliza nearly jumped out of her skin. "Sorry!"

"It's okay," Eliza shook off the fright, melting back into the leather seat.

"You're awfully jumpy," Esme observed, sliding into the seat beside her. "You okay?"

"Well, my sister fell overboard today and was gone for what seemed like hours," Eliza said. "I've never been more frightened in my life. Forgive me if I'm jumpy."

"I've seen you more frightened," Esme challenged, remembering the days she'd been a captive of the Night Doctor, and how desperate Eliza had been to find her. "But you didn't have to worry. Niko was with me."

"That's probably the only reason I didn't spiral into madness," Eliza admitted. "He seems like one of the good guys."

"He is," Esme stated, but the words sent a blush into her cheeks that Eliza could see even in the dim ship's lighting. Eliza had never seen her sister look like that.

"You like him?" Eliza stabbed a finger in her sister's arm. "Like, you like-like him?"

"What's not to like?" Esme admitted. "I mean, I hardly know him, but ... he's a skilled diver. He speaks Greek fluently. He's the one that translated the inscriptions in the grotto. I don't know why Aegis hasn't brought him in as an Agent. He could be a real asset. I might suggest it to So—" Esme stopped.

"Solan," Eliza said his name for her. "I wonder what will happen to him, especially if Father and Mother go to the Regents with what Elias said."

"How do you think Elias knew?" Esme asked.

"I haven't quite wrapped my brain around that one yet," Eliza said. "I mean, other than what he told me, there could be more to it than he knows. There could be a justifiable reason for Solan to have the Compass on his yacht. I'm not ready to pass judgement against him, but I would like answers."

"Is it really our place to demand answers from the Grand Aegis?" Esme asked the question Eliza hadn't considered.

"The Grand Aegis must be above reproach," Eliza said. "Perception is reality in many people's minds. He should know that. And maybe it's not our place, but Father and Mother will know the right thing to do."

"Well, that's a conversation for another day," Esme rose, stretching. "I'm exhausted."

"Sleep well," Eliza said, but didn't rise to follow.

"You should try to get some sleep, too. There's no telling what could happen tomorrow."

"I suppose you're right." Eliza stifled a yawn. She rose and followed her sister.

It was after midnight when the seas calmed enough for the tender to approach *The Pleiades* silently. The small engine on the trolling motor was electric, and thus, nearly silent as the rubber craft came alongside the yacht. There was a dim red light in the control room high above, but Charmaine had been watching for movement through her binoculars as they approached, and no one stirred. If the captain or his assistant were on duty, it was likely they'd nodded off, lulled by the gentle seas. That, or—if she knew Baxter—the captain had his nose in a book. Of course the strange behavior of *The Pleiades* left everything up in the air. The ship sat just outside the one mile radius of the island's forbidden zone, but it hadn't moved since the Wren girl returned with the safety diver.

Charmaine pointed at Corrine as she lashed the tender to *The Pleiades*, indicating she should stay, then summoned Rhea to follow her. As they'd discussed on their own boat, no one would speak to avoid alerting anyone on Solan's yacht of their presence. Silently, Charmaine and Rhea climbed aboard.

Charmaine knew exactly where to go. Keeping low, she led the way up the deck to the spiral staircase that led past the guest cabins and the VIP suite, to the owner's cabin where Solan had his office. She had a copy she'd made of his key, but was surprised when the door opened without it. *Had he left it unlocked?* He never left his cabin unlocked. It wasn't a good sign.

Once the door was closed behind them, Charmaine turned and lifted her torch to the bookcase by his desk—and froze.

The Compass was gone.

15

Charybdis

The night was still save for the gentle *shushing* of the sea against the hull when the first sound pricked at the edges of Eliza's consciousness ... the soft, metallic click of a latch being eased open and the soft grate of hinges rubbing against each other.

Eliza's eyes snapped open. Years of restless sleep had trained her to wake at the faintest disturbance. She listened, her breath shallow. Another sound followed: the faint creak of footfalls in the hall, far too cautious to be her family and out of place for the crew. She rose and pulled fuzzy socks on so that she could pad silently down the passage.

The door to Solan's cabin stood ajar, and a sliver of light from a phone torch sliced through the darkness. Two shadows moved within—one near the bookcase and one by the desk.

Eliza's voice cut through the darkness as she pushed the door open and flipped the lightswitch simultaneously. "Looking for something?"

Charmaine spun, eyes wide, as a single curl fell from her ponytail. Beside her, a woman who looked quite a lot like Charmaine—a sister, probably—froze. The shock on their faces lasted only a moment before both women straightened and masks of composure slipped into place.

"Eliza," Charmaine began smoothly, "you startled us."

"I'll bet I did. And I'm sure you have a marvelous explanation." Eliza crossed her arms over her chest and squared her stance, making retreat for the intruders problematic.

Charmaine stepped in front of Rhea, a subtly protective action, but her voice was smooth with a ready lie. "Solan asked me to verify something in his navigational data ... an anomaly. We—I—thought it best not to awaken anyone."

"So you snuck onto the yacht and broke into his cabin?" Eliza raised her voice, hoping that her family would wake and come to investigate. She was rewarded by the sound of opening doors and footsteps behind her.

"I ... had authorization," Charmaine replied. "We were just—"

"Checking in his bedroom?" Simon's tone was thick with insinuation.

A flicker of something darker than annoyance crossed Charmaine's features. "He keeps certain documents here. Sensitive ones. We didn't want to alert anyone."

Eliza's gaze was sharp. "I see. And what about her? Were you going to divide this 'navigational data' between you?"

Esme huffed behind her, a sound of amusement. "Sensitive docs, my arse cheek." Eliza felt her slip away, no doubt to alert the crew.

Rhea shifted her weight, guilt in her posture. "We weren't here to stir up trouble. We were just—"

"Just looking for something you expected to be on that shelf, I'll wager." Eliza's voice was quiet, dangerous.

Charmaine's mask slipped for an instant—just long enough to reveal the panic tucked behind it.

"Simon, Beatrice, I assure you this is all a misunderstanding."

"It always is, until it isn't," Beatrice responded icily.

Esme slipped into the salon and up the crew access staircase to the wheelhouse, where Bax sat at the wheel, eyes staring blankly out the windshield. He jumped when Esme appeared, and an earbud clattered to the floor.

"Esme, you surp—"

"We have intruders aboard," she interrupted him. "Charmaine and some other tall lass are in Solan's cabin rifling about."

The captain's eyes widened, his audio book forgotten. "Why wouldn't she let us know she was coming aboard?"

"Maybe because she'd rather sneak around with her torch in Solan's cabin ..."

Bax's eyes grew hard. "If she snuck aboard, then she's got a tender tied up somewhere." He rose from his seat and opened a small locker on the side of the helm station, drawing out a black plastic case.

"Is that a—"

"Flare gun, Miss Esme. Stay behind me. I don't want to accidentally blind you."

She nodded and they took the crew stairs back to the access door used for provisioning. Bax put his finger to his lips as he turned the handle a millimetre at a time. He pushed the door open, peeking out to see if another tender was visible along the starboard side. Seeing none, he crouched low and motioned for Esme to follow.

As they reached the cockpit, he stopped her and pointed toward the port edge of the stern. The bobbing edge of a tender was just visible over the transom. The two of them stepped soundlessly into the cockpit and squatted so low that they were practically crawling as they moved toward the hidden boat.

Bax counted out a 3-2-1 with his fingers and then popped up on the port stern, aiming the flare gun at the tender below. A third woman chirped in alarm and dropped her hold on *The Pleiades*.

Esme, anticipating such a move, had snagged the rescue pole from its harness along the side railing and used the loop to hook the oar lock on the small craft. "Oh, no you don't," she quipped.

"You'll come aboard," Bax insisted. "Now."

The third member of Charmaine's clandestine team blew out a breath, defeated.

The air in the salon pulsed with tension.

Beatrice folded her arms, staring at the three sisters. "You will explain yourselves. All of you."

Charmaine hesitated, then glanced at her sisters. Rhea was fidgeting with her necklace, as she always did when she was nervous. Esme followed Charmaine's gaze, then looked from one sister to the other. The younger Wren gasped as her eyes registered three ruby nautilus pendants. She turned back to Charmaine.

"Your necklace! I noticed it last year. But you all have them! Where did you get them?"

Charmaine's jaw twitched as she answered carefully. "I told you before. It was a gift from my grandmother. She gave them to each of us. Each woman in our line receives one on her eighteenth birthday. It's tradition."

"They look just like this …" Esme reached for the chain around her neck and produced the Ruby Nautilus from the grotto from beneath her pajama top.

Eliza sucked in a breath. "For pity's sake. You were *sleeping* with it on you, Ez?"

"Well, I thought that—"

A collective gasp from the sisters cut her short.

"Char, it's *real*!" one of the sisters exclaimed.

All eyes turned to the eldest sister. "It is indeed," Simon said, his voice measured. "Why don't you tell us all about it, Charmaine?"

Charmaine exhaled slowly, her eyes narrowed in disdain. "It's a relic. A *family* relic. A key to an inheritance you couldn't possibly understand."

"Oh, do give us a go," Beatrice hissed. "You'll find us a rapt audience."

"It belonged to one of our ancestors. A man named Timaeus. It's part of a larger Artifact."

"The Compass." Eliza watched the women's reactions. Charmaine flashed defiant, but her sisters, who she had introduced as Rhea and Corrine, kept their eyes on the edge of the rug.

"Yes, the Compass," Charmaine spat. "It belonged to Timaeus, too. The Ruby has been lost for millenia. It was said to guide the Compass home."

"Home?" Eliza's mind processed her history, searching for why the name Timaeus was familiar. It took her a second, but when the memory clicked, she gave a derisive snort. "Home *to Atlantis*? You expect us to believe that?"

"Believe what you wish. The Ruby is the heart of the Compass."

"Home is where the heart is," Esme said absently, and it was all Eliza could do not to groan. "The Compass wants to go home? Is that why it brought us here?"

"Esme, my dove, perhaps you should refrain from giving additional information to our interlopers here?" Simon suggested reproachfully, but Esme was on her own train of thought.

"It came here for the Ruby. She wanted me to find it." Eliza kicked Esme's ankle before she could reveal that *she* didn't refer to Charmaine or her sisters.

Charmaine didn't miss a beat. "It came here? As in the Compass brought you? Is that why you left Malta in the middle of the night?"

"It's a good thing I was on watch, or we wouldn't have been able to find you," Rhea offered, proud of her contribution to the adventure.

"Bloody hell, Rhea." Charmaine snapped. "You're as blabbermouthed as Esme." Rhea promptly resumed staring a hole in the rug. Charmaine turned back to Eliza as though the interruption had never happened. "The Compass took control of *The Pleiades*?"

Eliza nodded once, but remained silent.

"That makes total sense, actually." A spark gleamed in her eyes as though she'd just connected two very important dots. "You know—" Her voice slithered with charm and persuasion. "—we may well be on the same side of this. For years, I've tried to figure out a way to secure our birthright, and kept it a secret from the Order, even Solan. *Especially* Solan. People just aren't as trustworthy as we want them to be, are they?"

Eliza felt her eyes tighten at the aspersion cast toward the Order's Grand Aegis. Her own loyalty was faltering in light of the discovery of the Compass in his quarters. Charmaine noticed the fleeting doubt in Eliza's eyes and doubled down.

"You know as well as anyone how hard it is to be respected in something that was founded as a patriarchal organization, don't you? You too, Beatrice. For all the Order's high talk, women still struggle for the recognition our male counterparts get. I know every detail from every meeting that

Solan attends. I manage his schedule, his contacts ... hell, I even write his speeches sometimes. I work harder than anyone, and know the Archives better than anyone other than Randall. But did I get promoted to Leadership when a spot became available? No, I did not. Solan said he couldn't function without me. So because I'm good at my damn job, I'm stuck being the Administrative Assistant to a vain fool who would be little more than a figurehead if I didn't keep him on track. How is that fair?"

Beatrice put a hand on Eliza's shoulder. "It's true that women still have to fight certain stereotypes and biases to get our due, Charmaine. But you underestimate Solan. He's not a perfect man, but I've known him for probably your entire lifetime. He deeply loves the Order."

Charmaine snorted. "Not so much that he wouldn't use an Artifact or two for his own benefit. Do you know why he has the Compass on this boat? So his precious prize won't sink. That doesn't really seem to be for *the greater good*, does it?"

"And whose idea was it to bring the Compass here?" Beatrice asked pointedly. Charmaine's glare answered the question without the need for words. "I wonder what else you've talked him into, hmm?"

"It didn't take much persuasion, if you want to know the truth. And I needed the Compass here. Like I said, we may be on the same side, even if we don't agree about how we arrived. I know why the Compass came here." Her sisters sucked in their breath.

"For the Ruby," Esme said. "That's obvious."

"But do you know *why*? Do you know what it does?"

"We thought it best not to experiment with paired Artifacts," Eliza answered.

Charmaine chuckled, but there was no mirth in it. "Ah, so you've figured out one of the primary laws governing magic, have you?"

"That sounds like something a Covenant Operative would say," Esme snarled, but something clicked in Eliza's brain.

"It's magical physics," she muttered. "Duality. Action and reaction."

Charmaine nodded emphatically. "Says one of the two turtle doves."

A fire of understanding blazed through Eliza's head. "You know what it does?"

"Psht. Of course I do. It's my—our—legacy. Let me see it."

Simon shot a warning look, but Eliza—torn between reason and curiosity—turned and retrieved the Compass from a cabinet behind the settee. She placed it on the table.

The air shifted. The brass gleamed as though lit from within.

Charmaine's eyes burned. "You have no idea what power it holds."

"Then enlighten us," Eliza said.

"Gladly."

Before anyone could react, she snatched the pendant from around Esme's neck and clicked it into the center of the Compass. The metal sang a pure and sonorous note. The Ruby locked into place with a flash like crimson lightning.

The yacht lurched violently. Lights flickered and Simon grabbed the edge of the table as the floor tilted beneath him.

There was an alarmed shouting from the bridge. "We're dropping! There's no water under us!"

Eliza looked toward the large windows of the salon as her stomach twisted. The stars were spinning, the horizon vanishing. The sea itself seemed to peel away, collapsing downward in a spiral of black and silver.

The Compass blazed, its Ruby swirling with scarlet light, and a wind howled through the salon, though every window and door was sealed.

Esme's voice was a whisper in the chaos. "We're not falling. We're being swallowed!"

Then *The Pleiades* was engulfed by the darkness.

16

Turning the Tides

Eliza dreamt of the sea. But to her, it was a nightmare. She observed the sharks that circled in the muted moonlight illuminating the sea as she was dragged down into the darkness. She struggled for breath. There were creatures that should never exist anywhere but her dreams, creatures with scaly hands that grasped her arms and held her as she struggled to escape. Large fishy eyes stared out of human-like faces, gills behind their jaws, and bodies like her own, except for the legs. They had none. Nor did they have tails like mermaids. Instead, their lower bodies were like seahorses or snakes—eels perhaps— with gossamer thin fins along the sides that flickered and drew them deep into the abyss.

She tried to scream, but the sound of her own voice was lost in the expanse of the Mediterranean. Then came the maelstrom of swirling water, a vortex of such force that she felt as if she'd been torn from her own time and place.

Heavy-headed, she rose from the darkness, sitting up and gazing out over what should have been the salon in *The Pleiades,* but instead, was a sandy beach, littered with shells and stones. She gazed up, but found no sky. No moon. No stars. The expansive cavern reminded her of the grotto Esme described, but she hadn't mentioned it being so large.

Waves lapped at her socks that were now drenched, as was she. She shivered as she made her way onto unsteady feet. She launched herself forward as her mother crawled from the sea and collapsed on the beach ten metres from her. Her father appeared behind his wife, and Esme's head appeared in the water beyond the shore.

"Mother," Eliza helped Beatrice onto dry land. "are you hurt?"

"No," Beatrice coughed, catching her breath. "Help your father."

Eliza turned to find Simon as he got to his feet. "I'm fine." He waved her off.

Eliza stood, scanning the sea and the scene around them. She realized Esme wasn't the only one in the water. Charmaine and her accomplices broke the surface, surrounded by the same fishy-eyed creatures she'd dreamt of. Baxter, Amalie, Mateo, and Niko were surrounded, too.

The water behind them began to boil and churn, and the men seemed to sense a need for urgency to reach the dry land. Good thing, for just as the company cleared the cove, *The Pleiades* surfaced, rolled upright, and settled on the water as if nothing had happened.

Esme reached the beach, just in time to catch Eliza as her knees buckled, taking Esme down with her. "Eliza?"

"What was that?" the elder sister muttered.

Esme sat on her rump in the sand, watching as the rest of their party made it to the shore, looking like survivors of some horrid apocalypse, escorted to shore by some alien version of merfolk. The creatures were strong-bodied, like Amazons, though their lower half reminded Esme more of Echidna, the half-snake she-viper of Greek mythology, or maybe the Naga of Chinese lore. They were armed with spears, tridents, and lances. Clearly, they were a force to be reckoned with.

"Is everyone okay?" Baxter's commanding voice echoed in the void of the cavern that surrounded them.

"Eliza's a little shaken up," Esme said. "But I think we all are."

"Ssssilence!" one of the fish-eyed, snake-like merfolk commanded. The creature pointed to Eliza with his trident. "You."

Esme moved in front of her sister, protecting her, ready for a fight.

"You." It pointed at Esme, then turned his trident to Beatrice. "You."

Eliza managed to get to her feet, moving closer to her sister. Beatrice did the same, but not before Simon stepped forward. "What do you want with us? What is this place?"

The merman lifted his hand in a grand sweeping gesture, a hissing sound erupted from its chest. Simon was borne aloft, cast aside as the creature focused on the Wren women. "You are chossssen. Championssssss of Calypsssssoooo."

The creature moved closer. Eliza backed up, pulling Esme with her. Beatrice stood her ground, even as the undine moved within feet of her, gazing down as if in challenge. "What is the meaning of this?" Beatrice demanded.

"The Compassssss. The Cryssstal." The merman's eyes went to Eliza and Esme. "You. Reunited them."

Charmaine approached, fists clutched at her side, her wet curls brushed back off her high brow. "I'm the one that reunited the Artifacts. I joined them together."

The massive Naga moved so fast Eliza almost missed it. Charmaine stumbled back as his face came but inches from hers. "Silencccce!" the creature roared. "You are not chossssen. You are not championssssss."

Everyone seemed to back up as the creature rose to his full height supported by his tail. The spines that almost seemed like horns on his skull rose to their full glory. His chest seemed to broaden.

"Calm yourself, Narayan." A voice came from the water behind him. Eliza craned her neck to see a dark shadow patrolling the depths between land and *The Pleiades. Shark!* She took another step back.

"Take the others back to the ship. I will have a word with my champions." A fin broke the water, and Eliza felt light-headed. Esme noticed and caught her arm, holding her steady, even as she pressed back away from the water.

The merfolk army moved in, encircling the hapless victims of the unlikely shipwreck as a dark form swam beneath the shimmering waters. Eliza, Esme and Beatrice were cut off by two of the soldiers as the others were gathered in a circle. Narayan, who must have been the commander of this militia, laid his trident on the surface of the sand. It solidified, creating a half-wall that rose and encircled the crew of *The Pleiades*. Simon started for the wall to climb over, and was cuffed on the back of his head for his efforts.

"No!" Charmaine shoved her way past one of the soldiers. "I am the one that put the pieces together! The Artifact belongs to my sisters and me! We are the last of our Atlantean bloodline! It should, by all rights, be ours. We should be the champions!"

Narayan started to intercept her, but the voice from beneath the waters rose again. "She speaks truth, but the Compass and the Ruby belong to no one. Such power cannot be owned, only mastered."

"Then *I* will master it," Charmaine stomped her foot in the wet sand, splashing Beatrice in the effort.

The figure beneath the water circled back, growing larger as it morphed into something else. The water churned around it, and when it broke the surface, it wasn't a shark, it was a woman. Dressed in a robe of pale blue with a gold circlet around her head, she moved like a member of the royal family as she emerged from the sea. Esme's sharp intake of air startled her and Eliza didn't know if she should bow or prostrate herself. Clearly, this creature was at least royalty of some sort.

Her eyes were as blue as the Mediterranean, and her hair fell behind her shoulders in long dark waves that dried almost as quickly as her clothing. "Good Lady Wren," the creature bowed to Beatrice. "I am Calypso."

Beatrice glanced over the nymph's shoulder, meeting Simon's eye, sending a silent message of assurance. "My daughters, Eliza and Esme."

"They are known to me." Calypso nodded to each of them. "For an eternity and a day, I have been banished from my home. When your daughters found my Artifacts, I knew you were worthy to serve me. I must employ you to aid me in my challenge."

"We serve at the pleasure of the Grand Aegis," Beatrice said. "Do you know of our Order?"

"You—and your Order—are known to the Council of Seven," the nymph said, "But the Council has wronged me, and I will have my challenge heard."

"The Council of Seven?" Esme asked.

"The Immortals that watch over your factions, the purveyors of Fate who have denied me the right to return to my home."

"Your home?"

"Long before the seas swallowed my homeland, before the sky cracked and the veil between worlds was drawn, I served the Tidelord as the keeper of currents. Neither immortal nor mortal, I was sworn to guide and protect travelers who honored the old ways. But I was blinded by love for a traveler and offered him immortality and eternal youth if he would only agree to stay with me." She spoke as a woman still in love, and Eliza's thoughts went to Phillip, safely back at Pompeii, happy in his work. "But he was a sailor, a traveler. The sea was his first love, and I knew I could only win his heart by letting him go. So, I crafted a Compass to protect him, and forged the heart from my own blood and tears, so that together, the two would guide him safely back to me when he was ready for my love."

"What happened?" Beatrice asked, though the tale rang familiar.

"He returned to his *wife*." Her tone turned sharp, bitter. "When next he dared to enter my realm, I took my rage and my heartbreak out upon his ships. I summoned the maelstrom and turned the tides against him. It angered his patron, who was a powerful goddess in her own right. It was a betrayal I would regret, for my love for him was great and it was my hand that nearly ended his life. As a result, I was cast out from my home, and forced to travel the endless sea, but before I could gain the gods' forgiveness, the rift between man and gods grew into war, and my island, my home, was consumed by the sea. Only one survived the cataclysm, a sailor who escaped with *my* Compass, and *my* Ruby."

Eliza leaned close to her sister and whispered, "Does this story sound familiar?"

Esme nodded, "*The Odyssey*?"

Eliza confirmed the thought with a simple nod.

"I became *Calypso the Unmoored*. *The Nymph Between Worlds*. For ages, I have sought a way back, but the Rift cannot be crossed by strength or sorrow. Only the Council of Seven—the ancient arbiters who govern the boundaries between divine realms—have the authority to open the passage again. They demand a challenge. A reckoning."

"How is this *our* battle?" Beatrice asked, keeping her tone soft and unchallenging.

"There is a prophecy," Calypso said, dipping her finger into the placid waters, she drew a symbol and the water shimmered, casting a light on the ceiling of the grotto. "When the Compass stirs and Crystal wakes, three shall be called to challenge the Gate."

Modern legends say the ancient city was consumed by the sea in a single night. But the truth was revealed before their eyes. An image of an ancient city appeared, consumed by a wave not of water but of dimensional energy. It showed Calypso escorted away by the fishy-faced army, held back and unable to aid her people, as the lone castaway—Timaeus—escaped the destruction in a flimsy craft, carrying the only two remaining Artifacts of a civilization destroyed in a single night—a Compass and a Ruby.

Calypso continued.

"One of mind, one of will, one of truth,
To face the challenge, provide the proof.
Before the Seven their vows are tied
To bind the breach and calm the tide.
Fail, and the depths claim their due.
Prevail, and the waters reveal what's true.
Only when the challenge is met
Can the nymph repay her debt."

"I still don't understand what this has to do with us," Esme said, flatly.

"You are known to the Council of Seven, as are the other women who traveled here with you tonight," she said. "There are factions at odds, much as the Fathers favor the Order of Aegis or the Covenant of Obsidian. While they are tasked with observing and mandated to remain neutral, everyone knows this is not how the game is played. Sometimes, you have to force Fate's hand, for we must all answer to it."

"And if we refuse?" Eliza found her voice.

Calypso's face darkened, as her eyes narrowed. "Refusal means death. For us all."

The nymph reached a hand down into the water, and it churned around her, the water turning red as blood. When she withdrew her hand, she held the Compass, with the glowing Ruby throbbing in a tempo that matched

Eliza's pulse. "Now you have brought me the last piece I need to make my challenge and so ... it begins."

She lifted the Compass over her head, a rumbling shook the grotto, and a piercing scream forced the human women to cup their hands over their ears.

"Council of Seven, hear me! I am Calypso the Unmoored, cast out by the Rift and bound to foreign tides. I invoke my right of petition! By ancient law and living tide, I demand the Challenge of Return. Let the chosen stand. Let the Gates be opened. By the laws set before the tides turned against me, I claim the Trial of Return! Let the chosen stand in my stead as my champions. I demand you judge truth from shadow! Hear the voice you cast away! By ancient covenant and forgotten law I demand my right to a trial by contest. Let your judgement fall, and my passage home be granted!" The nymph's voice rose to the highest peak of the cavernous ceilings, stalactites crumbled and showered down, splashing in the water, striking the soft soil around the women as they ducked and threw their arms over their heads.

The rocks themselves seemed to shift, as the sky appeared above them, black as ink, dappled in brilliant skies. The grotto was now a colosseum—an amphitheatre. Eliza stood, glancing at her mother and sister as her eyes lifted to scan the scene. A single figure sat in each of seven stone sections that reminded her of box seats at the opera, but Eliza couldn't discern the individual features of each of the Seven.

One of the figures stood. "Who dares summon the Council of Seven? A lowly nymph? How dare you call this committee to order?"

"It is my right," Calypso answered. "For the centuries of service I have provided to the gods, I have received only torment and sorrow. I beseech the Council. Will no one support my claim?"

A second figure to Eliza's left rose. A wizened old man stepped forward, leaning heavily on a staff with a crystal orb perched atop it. "I will support your claim, child. You have made a wise choice of Champions. May the gods be in your favor." His quavering voice felt familiar to Eliza.

"So be it." The head of the Council spoke flatly, but Eliza could sense he was put off by the whole affair. "A Challenge of Return is no challenge without opposition. Recognizing this nymph's right to contest, who will choose champions to oppose them?"

"I will," a woman rose from her seat and leaned on the rail before her. She was a beautiful creature, with long flowing red hair. She wore a gown as thin as a butterfly's wing, but in muted tones. A serpent coiled around her shoulders and wrapped itself around her wrist. Her dark eyes glinted as if illuminated by flames. They shone so bright Eliza could make them out, even from the beach below. "There are three daughters of Atlantis present in this chamber. Three who have every right to contest the claim of this nymph. Bring them forth and let them serve as the Defenders of the Gate."

"So it is to be done," the head of the Council lifted a hand, and bowed to the woman, then to the old man. "Let the Challenge begin."

17

ADRIFT

The deck of the *Naxos* rocked gently beneath their feet, the boards creaking like they resented the extra weight. Phillip emerged from the empty v-berth cabin and joined Elias in the wheelhouse, his eyes scanning the early morning horizon and the jagged silhouette of Filfla bathed in pale sunlight.

"No sign of them or why they were following *The Pleiades*," Phillip said.

Elias checked the AIS display screen on the bulkhead—still lit, still transmitting. "This is the right boat. Same MMSI the rental company gave us. Good thing they had a GPS tracker installed on board to keep track of their assets." Concern laced through his matter-of-fact tone and he ran his hand through his hair in exasperation.

Phillip huffed a mirthless laugh. "I'm still amazed they handed over the coordinates just because we sounded worried enough."

"They only caved because they couldn't reach Charmaine. Eight missed calls, two voicemails, and four texts. They were starting to panic. They're a small company and didn't have enough manpower to search for *Naxos* themselves."

"Plus your very convincing 'my dear friend is lost at sea' routine," Phillip muttered.

Elias didn't bother denying it. "Worked, didn't it?"

Phillip scanned the helm controls. Everything was in neutral and powered down, save for the AIS system that would ensure a larger boat didn't plow over *Naxos* in the dark.

"I guess they must've anchored outside the Valletta port," Phillip went on, "or else the harbor master there would have had a record of them."

Elias nodded. "Agreed. Which is why we had to cold-call every rental agency in Salerno to find out who hired *Naxos* out." He allowed himself a brief smile. "Your first three explanations were terrible, by the way."

Phillip stiffened. "Excuse me?"

"Who tells a rental clerk, 'my friend must have gone off for a moonlit swim ...' Honestly, Phillip."

Phillip rolled his eyes. "Okay, fine. But *your* lie was better?"

"It got results."

Phillip had to concede the point. "Fine. But I'd still like to know how you got Charmaine's personal cell phone number."

Elias didn't answer at first. He ran his thumb along the teak rail, his jaw tightening. "We have ... history," he said finally.

Phillip looked like he wanted to press the point, but the silence in the air between them felt too brittle. Instead he motioned toward the small davit on the deck. "The tender is gone. They must've taken it somewhere."

"I'd lay dollars to donuts that if we find that tender, we find *The Pleiades.*" Elias used the radio to scan frequencies, but found only static.

"So whatever happened," Phillip said quietly, his voice taut, "we're already too late to stop it."

Elias stepped out of the wheelhouse and into the cockpit and stared toward Filfla. He felt a cold knot twist in his gut. "I don't accept that. This just makes it more complicated."

Phillip let out a measured breath. "So you agree that they're still out there. All of them."

"I know they are," Elias answered, though he lacked the conviction he tried to convey. "The question is *where*?"

Water folded away like a curtain being drawn, and suddenly Esme found herself in a chamber that felt as ancient as the sea itself.

"Where are we?" a voice asked, and Esme turned to see one of Charmaine's sisters—Rhea, if she recalled correctly—looking around in alarm.

The walls overhead curved into a perfect dome, white stone marbled with a blue phosphorescence. The blue light pulsed like the slow beating of a colossal heart. Esme slipped her sandals off, and the stone floor was warm beneath her feet. "The heart of the sea," Esme muttered, wiggling her toes as the lifeforce within the pavers tickled her.

Rhea put her hands on her hips and looked from Esme's face to her feet, then back again. "Oi, Char said you were an odd one. Can the floor tell you how to get out of here, then?"

"I suspect it could," Esme answered, "but I don't think that's the point."

Rhea gave an exasperated sigh, and Esme fixed her eyes on the gleaming object at the center of the room. A throne of coral and gold rose from the rock, grown rather than built. Its arms spiraled like auger shells, and the back was a lattice of pearlescent bone that shimmered faintly in the diffuse light.

Before the throne yawned a circular pit—wide, black, and impossibly still. It wasn't the darkness of shadow, nor the reflective depth of water. It was something else entirely: a void that swallowed light as though it fed on it.

Rhea gasped and stepped back instinctively, but Esme found herself leaning forward without meaning to.

Beyond the chamber walls, the water held their families like spectators behind a one-way mirror. Esme could just make out the silhouette of her mother with arms crossed, of Eliza pressed against the barrier, of Charmaine and Corrine on the far side, watching their sister intently.

The air trembled. A voice rose, not of sound waves, but of resonance, as if felt through the bones rather than the ears.

"To sit on the throne, one must know herself." The voice came from everywhere and nowhere at the same time. **"To know herself, she must confront the void."**

"What do you mean 'confront it?'" Rhea demanded. There was a faint hum in the air, and Esme thought it tasted like amusement.

Her breath caught. This wasn't a physical trial; it was something far worse. A test of the spirit, the soul. "Oh, bloody hell," Esme grumbled. "Crack on, then. At least it's not a tunnel." She took a deep breath and waited.

Rhea moved first. Charmaine's younger sister squared her shoulders and approached the pit with her chin lifted in a show of defiance, as though daring the darkness to challenge her. Only the trembling of her hands betrayed the truth of her fear. Esme found herself frozen in place, unable to do anything but watch as Rhea faced the darkness.

As Rhea peered into the void, the blackness shifted. One ripple, and then another. Swirling faces appeared on the surface: a man with a disapproving glare, Charmaine looking disappointed and shaking her head, a crown crumbling on a sandy beach, swallowed by waves. Then a shape formed—Rhea herself, draped in Atlantean blue, standing atop a gleaming terrace surrounded by adoring faces. Her sisters knelt beside her, not as equals, but as attendants. The image of Rhea smiled, radiant and regal.

She gasped. "Atlantis! It's showing me Atlantis!" Her fingers stretched forward, burning with the need to touch the vision. "It's the prophecy, just like Yiayia told us! And it's *me*! It called *me*! I'm the chosen in my bloodline! *Me*!"

Her hand still outstretched, Rhea froze in place and Esme felt the ability to move return to her limbs.

"The other must face the void," the voice boomed. "Then you must both choose."

Esme looked toward her family. Their faces were blurred by the water barrier, but she recognized Eliza's posture instantly—hands up, willing her sister to be brave. Beatrice stood behind her, anxious and helpless. On the far side, Charmaine's blurred face was pale, furious, terrified. Corrine paced back and forth beside her.

Esme drew a breath. The air tasted of salt and starlight. She stepped toward the pit, and the darkness shifted, welcoming her. Curiosity tugged at her. What visions would she see? She wanted to rush forward, imagining that she already had a kinship with the lifeforce of the chamber, but she moved slowly toward the void instead. She studied it, inspected it, acted cautiously, like Eliza would want her to do.

Images moved in the inky surface, and Esme squeaked in alarm as the first shapes formed.

Eliza, throat cut, pale and floating in the waters of the Mediterranean. Her parents, aging, grieving, broken. And then a vision of herself, alone, joyless, but standing on the dais of Atlantis, glowing with power.

"No ..." The word caught in her throat, cut off by a sob.

You can save them, the voice whispered in her mind. ***If you take the throne, the power to undo this future will be yours.***

Esme's gut twisted as adrenaline and fear pumped through her. There was nothing she wouldn't do to protect her family. She cast outward with her empathic senses, trying to feel Eliza and her mother, but was met only with a sizzling static. There would be no reassuring nudge from her sister, no clarifying vision to tell her what to do. She was well and truly on her own, with her family hanging in the balance.

Still, something in the set-up of this trial felt *wrong*. Esme tried to think like Eliza. *Analyze the problem, don't assume facts not in evidence. ASK QUESTIONS.*

"Why have you chosen me for this challenge?" she asked the disembodied voice. The more she thought about it, the less sense it made. Eliza would have been a better choice to take the throne—Esme had neither gift nor desire for leadership. And if this challenge was to decide who should sit on the throne, Beatrice was more regal than either of them. For that matter, why would Rhea be chosen instead of Charmaine? Esme's mind spun.

"Only one of the champions may claim the throne."

Rhea fell backward, unfrozen and free of the pit's spell. She clambered to her feet, and she and Esme stared at each other in confused and awkward silence.

"So ... do we fight for it, then?" Rhea asked.

"I don't know what we're supposed to do," Esme snapped. "I don't want the blasted throne. I don't want to fight you, either. But this doesn't feel right to me ..."

"Well, then ..." Rhea lunged for the throne, no hesitation.

Esme acted out of instinct, not to seize the throne, but to stop Rhea from making a rash and potentially catastrophic choice. She stepped between Rhea and her prize.

Rhea snarled, "Move! You don't want it—I do!"

"That's exactly why I can't let you take it." Esme squared her stance and, when Rhea attempted to push past her, redirected the woman's kinetic energy as they collided, just as Wally had taught her. The impact jarred her, helping her focus.

"I deserve it!" Rhea struggled to break free of Esme's grip. "I saw *me*! Atlantis chose *me*!"

"You saw what you wanted, not what was real!" She hadn't realized what she was saying until the words were out of her mouth. The vision of Eliza ... that hadn't been a real future either. It had been a flashback to the moment she thought she'd lost her sister.

Rhea, still not understanding, shrieked with rage. The surface of the void rippled, and tendrils of shadow rose from its black surface. They shaped themselves into ethereal tentacles, writhing toward Rhea's ankles. She let out a howl and struggled harder. As if reacting to her panic, the surface stretched wider, inching toward the women as they strained against each other.

"Stop, Rhea. You're feeding it. You're making it worse!" Esme shifted her position so that she had Rhea in a grip similar to a swimming rescue.

"You're trying to steal it from me! You want to throw me in so you can take it for yourself, you lying witch!"

A charcoal tentacle slithered toward Rhea's leg as she kicked and struggled. Then, fast as a cobra strike, it slapped itself against her bare calf, the suction cups pulsating as it drank in her fear.

"Quit fighting me, ya numpty!" Esme hollered. "I'm trying to get you to safety!" She planted her feet hard against the stone and hauled Rhea in the opposite direction, playing tug-of-war with the darkness.

With an audible *pop*, the tendril snapped free and retracted into the void. The girls tumbled to the ground in a heap of limbs, breathless.

Rhea pushed herself to her feet, and Esme followed suit. Charmaine's sister crouched, prepared to return to battle.

"No," Esme said simply. She raised her hands in surrender. "I'm not going to fight for something I don't want. I'm not going to fight to be someone I'm not. I'm not going to fight for a lie." She stepped away from the throne, clearing the path.

A rustling whisper echoed from the dome above, as though reacting to Esme's decision to yield. Rhea laughed breathlessly and raced for the throne.

As her hands connected with the delicately wrought armrest, the chamber convulsed. A torrent of black energy spiraled upward from the pit like a reversed whirlpool, emitting a powerful pulse that threw Rhea backward. She landed hard on her shoulder and cried out in shock and pain.

Esme, braced and calm, remained steady. "Stop reaching for something that isn't yours to take," she called to the prostrate woman. "You're hurting yourself."

Esme stepped forward, studying the throne's form, its artistry. From behind her, she heard Rhea begin to cry in frustration, but Esme was entranced by the beauty before her. The throne was a marvel of craftsmanship, as if grown from the sea rather than crafted by mortal hands. The coral arms, pale as bleached bone, curled outward in spirals reminiscent of nautilus shells, but it was the gilt work overlaying them that caught her breath.

Delicate filigree of hammered gold twined through the coral branches like living vines, impossibly thin and etched so finely that each tendril bore tiny reliefs of mythic scenes no larger than a fingernail. Some images she recognized: Poseidon and his great trident hovering over a storm-tossed ship in an angry sea, a maze of gold executed with mathematical precision ... but it was the image on the handrest that caught her attention.

Seven figures, each with a different celestial crown, sat in judgement over a rising tide.

Where the coral met the gold at the seat's edge, a large panel dominated the design—a sunken city, rendered in tiny geometric shapes. Golden towers leaned sideways, swallowed by stylized currents etched in whorls and crescents. Above it, a single figure—a woman diving headfirst into darkness—seemed to fall endlessly into the void below, her body sculpted so delicately that light shimmered across it like ripples reflecting sunlight.

Without thinking, Esme ran her fingertips gently across the image, understanding its meaning. "They cast you out," she muttered softly to no one in particular. "Left you behind."

Then Esme sat, not on the seat of the throne, but at the foot of it on the dais. And she wept for Calypso.

The throne pulsed softly.

"True power comes from wisdom, and true wisdom comes from knowing one's own heart. Esme Wren may pass."

The water walls of the chamber dissolved, and the spectators—Beatrice, Eliza, Charmaine, and Corrine—gasped as Esme was bathed in the throne's gentle light.

18

The Monster In the Maze

The window to the competition grounds went opaque but Eliza felt something in the room shift. She turned around to find Esme and Rhea standing behind them. She glanced over at Charmaine and noted the disapproval on the woman's face. Charmaine had always been polite to Eliza, but the expression directed at her defeated sister revealed a different side, one that was judgemental, overbearing, and definitely not happy.

Rhea turned away from her sister and leaned into Esme, saying something so faint Eliza couldn't hear it. Esme nodded and moved over to her sister and mother. "What was that?" Eliza asked.

"You could see it?"

"Yes. We saw the competition," Beatrice said. "But, what was that with Charmaine's sister?"

"Tell ya later," Esme said, fidgeting nervously. "Now what?"

Before anyone could answer, the room dimmed. Eliza found herself in the ring. A line from the movie *Beyond Thunderdome* resounded in her head. *Two men enter. One man leaves.* Esme had come back safely, so surely it couldn't be that bad, right? Corrine stood in the distance, luminous under the lighting that warmed the void around them.

The woman wasn't especially tall, nor especially lean, but she moved with a grace Eliza herself lacked. Corrine's jet-black hair, drawn up into a high ponytail curled ever-so-slightly around her long neck, resting on her shoulder. Not a hair out of place, unlike Eliza's haphazard braid that was thick, but limp down her back. Wisps of her mousy hair escaped around her face.

Eliza flinched as mirrors rose from the sands around her in every direction, trapping her in. She could feel the maze seal behind her with a sound like glass breathing. The walls were seamless, perfect, the mirrors impossibly deep. Eliza met her own reflection, recoiling at the sight. Her glasses sat askew on the bridge of her sunburnt nose. Her hair was worse than she expected. She hadn't slept well in so long that the dark circles around her eyes had become permanent. She looked frail. Weak.

"Know thyself as thou knowest thine enemy," a different male voice, this one deeper with a musical resonance, commanded from the void outside the maze. The mirrors trembled and fractured, splitting her image into a dozen versions of herself, each one slightly out of sync. **"Golems three await thee. Seek the truth, or turn and flee. Choose your weapons ... carefully."**

The ground seemed to tremble, and Eliza felt the game had begun, though she still didn't understand the rules or the objective.

She moved with tentative precision, counting steps, marking each turn as she moved, treating the challenge like a physics problem begging to be solved, allowing her right hand to remain on the wall, trusting that would lead her out.

The mirrors distorted depth perception, but not randomly. It left her feeling unsteady, but there was repetition. A method she tried to analyze.

The instructions ran through her mind, as she tried to make sense of them. *Choose your weapon carefully.* What did that mean?

Above the open-topped maze, she heard a shriek, the sounds of battle, then the clank of shattering glass. *Had Corrine found her first golem? Where were the weapons? Would she be strong enough to defeat a monster in the maze?*

The images of a minotaur hiding in the shadowed maze of the labyrinth flooded her mind. Lost in her imagination, she stumbled over something in her path, something she hadn't seen. Mirrored chains tangled in her feet and she went down hard. The landing knocked the air from her lungs. She rolled over and sat up, looking at the obstacle a moment before reaching to untangle herself. She held fast to the chains, thinking they might become useful.

Umbrae vocem audite ... anima fracta, redi ad nos ... Umbrae vocem audite ... Mortui te exspectant.

The voices caught her off guard.

No. No. No! Not now. I don't have time for this. Eliza froze, a shadow in the darkness. "Go away!" She covered her ears, whacking herself in the head with the chains still in her hand.

Umbrae vocem audite ... anima fracta, redi ad nos ... Umbrae vocem audite ... Mortui te exspectant.

She straightened and tried to shake off the troubling memories that came with the voices. *No. I'm not doing that right now!* She took a deep breath.

"I'm not asleep. I can control this." She let her mind go to a more pleasant place. *Phillip.* His voice soothed her as it had the other night on the phone. It gave her the calm she needed and drowned out the ominous voices that had followed her. She'd never been able to quiet the voices in her dreams.

Continuing on she finally found herself in a clearing. Eliza hesitated, but moved into the open, trying to calculate what might happen, looking for an alternative exit route in case she needed to run. Unlike Esme, a battle of strength would be a horrid challenge—one she didn't think she could win.

A green garden surrounded by mirrored walls held a statue surrounded by a clear fountain. Rose bushes encircled the marble retaining wall where small carved cherubs held vessels with water spilling out. It reminded her of a smaller version of the Navarinou fountain. The statue suddenly moved, and turned to face her. A bright smile passed over the golem's face, and Eliza gasped when it moved towards her, hopping down and wading through the water to reach her.

Eliza took a step back. "Phillip?" *Why? Why was he here? Was it because she was thinking of him?*

"I couldn't find you," he said. "We've been searching for days." He moved closer, but Eliza raised a hand to guard herself.

This isn't real, she reminded herself. "Why are you *here*?"

"Isn't it obvious?" Phillip reached for her, but she moved away. "I've been worried."

"You don't need to worry about me. I'm not some damsel that needs saving," Eliza said. "I'm fine."

He stopped, turning away. She studied him as he slipped his hand into his pocket, his head dropping. His chest heaved as he took in a breath. "I love you, Eliza. Yet, you continue to push me away. I can't keep chasing you through mirrors." He turned, facing her, his eyes red. "You treat love like it's a science experiment you expect to fail."

Eliza caught the flash of movement near his knee. He held a crystal blade in his hand, its crescent edge deadly-sharp. *No. This wasn't real. Phillip would never hurt her.*

But this wasn't Phillip.

He moved with lightning speed towards her, catching her off balance. She recovered quickly, dodging under the knife and putting distance between them. Her body tightened remembering the feel of Maelis's blade against her throat. She swallowed hard, trying to make sense of this whole scenario.

Why Phillip? Why?

Know thyself as thou knowest thy enemy. Phillip wasn't her enemy. Maybe they'd started off butting heads, but things had changed. Still, she had been exploring her own feelings. Testing the waters. Then it hit her. She *had* been treating their relationship like an experiment.

Define the variables:

1. How do I feel about Phillip?

2. Does my stress level increase or decrease around him?

3. Do I sleep better when I hear his voice?

4. Am I more distracted or focused?

Introduce Controlled Exposure:

1. One kiss, then distance.

2. One phone call, then a week of silence.

She'd been opening up to him in increments. Testing the stimuli and response.

Define The Exit Conditions:

1. I'm not making any promises.

2. Let's see where this goes.

3. I don't know what it means yet.

But she did know. All the data aligned. She'd been moving closer to the irreversible change. No, she hadn't *fallen* in love with him. She'd tested it. Carefully. Incrementally. She'd been hoping all the results would be conclusive, and they were.

She *was* in love with Phillip.

He charged again, and Eliza stepped quickly. Without thinking, she flipped the chain in her hand over the blade, yanking hard. He passed, the blade grazing her cheek as it came down.

Spinning, she flipped the chain over him, drawing him in, pulling him closer to her, so close the blade couldn't reach her again.

Breathless, she pulled him into her, their lips only inches apart. "I don't want to fight."

"You already know how this ends," he spoke softly, his breath warm against her skin. "You're just afraid to admit your choice. As if you want this to fall apart so you don't have to choose."

"I choose you. I choose love," Eliza lifted herself up on her tiptoes and pressed her lips to his.

The golem shattered around her, and fell into shards at her feet.

There was no fanfare, no cheers, nothing to tell her if she'd made the right choice. Eliza staggered back, somewhat relieved, but afraid of what might be next. She glanced at the chains in her hand, and let them fall away, noticing the crystal blade laying on the ground. Eliza picked it up, studying her own blood on the mirrored surface. Her hand went to her cheek, and came back sticky.

"Eliza?" she heard Esme's voice in the maze. *What was she doing here?* She'd already completed her trial. Eliza hurried into the fractured glass hallway, moving cautiously, with her hand raised to avoid crashing into an unseen wall. The reflection of herself no longer appeared, making the maze all the more dizzying and dangerous to traverse.

"Esme? Where are you?"

"Eliza! Help me!" Her sister's voice screamed of fear and pain. Eliza was certain of the turn when she reached the end of the corridor, and found herself facing Esme, blocking the path with a split-head spear.

"Haha! You're mine now!" the Esme-golem stabbed verbally before the attack.

Off guard, Eliza was helpless. The spear missed her on the initial lunge, but grazed her as the golem pulled it back, prepared to strike again. Eliza got her own blade between them, parrying against the onslaught.

"Esme, what is this? I've never done anything to hurt you."

"Oh, yeah?" Esme grunted, lunging again. Eliza danced backwards, narrowly avoiding the piercing this aberration intended. "You promised you'd never hurt me ... but you chose *him* over me."

"Him?" Eliza puzzled. "What are you talking about?"

"We've been a team since the beginning," Esme sneered, advancing. "But you'd rather be with Phillip than me? Don't think I don't know you'd rather have him for a partner. Why do you think I've been training so hard? So you'd pick me. I can't do this alone."

"Esme, no," Eliza protested, knowing her real sister would never say such things. "You're not just my sister. You're my best friend. I would never allow you to go into danger if I wasn't there to back you up."

Eliza realized she'd been backed into a corner. She had nowhere else to go. The Esme-golem knew that too, and a wicked grin appeared on its face. It drew back its spear and prepared to charge. With no other choice, Eliza straightened, dropping her weapon in surrender. "I can't defeat you," she said. "And I won't hurt you. Ever."

"You may regret that some day," the golem said, then shattered, collapsing into a pile of light.

Eliza collapsed back against the wall, mentally and physically exhausted, the hooked blade dropping from her hand, clanging against the floor beside the spear the Esme-golem had wielded. Two weapons. *Which should she choose?*

The spear had a clear advantage, and Esme might have bested her with it if she hadn't made the choice not to fight. So, ignoring the blade, she picked up the spear. She leaned against it for a moment, taking a deep breath.

Again, the sound of combat echoed above the maze, and she knew Corrine had faced her second golem. Urged on, Eliza gathered herself, steeled her courage and advanced through the maze without looking back.

Eliza wandered in the maze for what seemed like hours. Lost in the intricate web of halls and dead ends. The morass of darkness seemed to be closing in, when she found what appeared to be the exit. Outside the maze stood the third golem, a statue on a dais.

Circling the unmoving figure, she discovered this creature wore Elias's face.

Not a mask of the monster she perceived him to be. It was the brother she'd once trusted. Eliza nearly jumped out of her skin when its head turned and it smiled. It reached for her chin, cupping it, taking Elias's full form. "You should have known," it said gently in her brother's voice. "I would never betray you."

Her breath caught. "This isn't real. You're ... an echo."

The golem tilted his head. "Then why does it still hurt?"

"Why did you do it? Why did you betray us? Aegis? Our parents? Esme?" She felt tears building in her eyes. She knew this wasn't real, but she couldn't help it. "Me?"

“You think I betrayed you? I chose a truth I thought you could survive. Some betrayals are just sacrifices seen from the wrong side.”

“The wrong side?” Eliza felt heat burn in her eyes as he moved behind her. Circling her.

“I loved you enough to let you hate me,” he said. “You were never the thing I betrayed.”

“It sure felt like betrayal,” Eliza snapped.

The golem took her hand, locking eyes with her. "You only see what they tell you to see, Eliza."

Eliza yanked her hand away, and backed up, lowering the spear between them. “Draw your weapon and let’s get this over with.”

Elias stood fast, lowering his hands and stretching them out at his side. “No weapons, Eliza. That’s not why I’m here.”

“No!” Eliza’s voice broke as she screamed the word. The damage from Maelis’s blade had healed, but it didn’t hurt any less now. “You lie! You’re a liar.”

“If I hadn’t,” Elias spoke softly. “You’d be dead.”

That landed harder than any blow. Eliza raised the spear and stabbed blindly at him. “You left!” Tears burned in her eyes and mixed with the blood on her cheek. “You chose them.”

“I left,” he corrected, dancing out of her aim, “so you wouldn’t follow. But you did. *You* made that choice.”

She shook her head, the motion sharp and angry. “You don’t get to make those kinds of decisions for me.”

“I already did,” Elias said. “And you’re still standing.”

Eliza’s breath came in panting gasps, her hands trembling, tears blurring her vision as she lifted the spear again. “You think this absolves you?” she demanded. “A few truths wrapped in pretty words?”

"No," he stated flatly. "I think you want me to be the villain, so you don't have to forgive yourself."

Her breath hitched. "For what?"

"For not trusting me when it mattered."

"I don't trust you now," she stated flatly, charging at him. "You betrayed us." The spear in her grasp pulled at her, as if yearning to attack.

Elias held her blurred gaze. She charged and drove the spear hard. It sent a vibrating pain through her hands and up her arms as it made contact, pulling her in as Elias went down, impaled. She lay on top of him, feeling the shaft of the spear against her own abdomen.

Elias wheezed. "I did not betray you. That is ... the truth."

She searched his face for the tell. The crack. The lie.

"Knowing when to trust, and when to fight is the key to victory, Corrine Andrews may pass."

Eliza glanced up as Corrine appeared from the exit of the maze disheveled, but victorious. But wait ... she had bested Elias in battle. *How could she have lost?* She glanced down and found the golem gone, the spear on the ground beneath her, saturated in blood.

Only then did she realize her mistake. Elias *was* telling the truth.

19

The Great Unmaking

A heavy sigh in her ear startled Beatrice.

"I had hoped for a different outcome for Eliza," Calypso breathed. "Now it is all up to you, I'm afraid."

Beatrice Wren turned to look at the sea nymph, but found no body accompanying the voice. She scanned the cavern and felt her shoulders loosen in relief as Eliza emerged through an archway, her expression distant and disturbed. Esme rushed to her sister's side and hugged her close.

Bea started toward them, and nearly tripped. Looking down, she was startled to find that the Compass, complete with shimmering Ruby, lay at her feet. Without thinking, she bent down and picked up the ancient Artifact.

A sound like a thousand chimes fracturing at once echoed through the cavern.

The chamber rumbled and shook, as though the heart of the earth itself had roared. Cracks spiderwebbed across the stone floor, glowing with scarlet light.

Eliza cried out as the floor shattered beneath her feet. A crevasse opened, and she and Esme slid helplessly into the gap in the broken stone. Their mother charged forward, hoping to grab hold of them, but the trembling ground kept her off balance. With a wail, Beatrice forced herself to look into the jagged crack, afraid of the sight that might greet her eyes.

She fell to her knees in relief to see her girls, backs to the wall, atop a narrow ledge.

They were out of reach, but they were safe.

For now.

Esme's terrified gaze found her mother first. "Mum! We're okay!"

Eliza was already studying the sheer face of the crevasse. "There are no edges we can use to climb. You'll have to find—" She was interrupted as another tremor brought a rain of fist-sized rocks.

"Can you sit?" Bea asked them. "I don't want you to lose balance and pitch over the edge. I'll get help!" Her daughters pressed their backs hard into the wall and sat carefully. "Just hold tight, lovelies. It'll be alright!" She tried to sound confident, but her heart was in a panic.

A quick survey of the chamber told her that there was nothing she could lower into the crack to try and help them climb out. "Calypso! Anyone! Help!" she called out, hoping the immortal beings were close enough to hear her. "Esme and Eliza are in trouble! We need help!"

Beatrice felt the vibrations beneath her feet a fraction of a second before the next massive tremor hit. Above her head, the marble dome shattered, raining debris down upon her head. On the opposite side of the chamber, the wall ripped open as more cracks laced outward.

Beyond the ruined wall, rising towers of quartz and gold shimmered in diffuse sunlight.

Atlantis.

Not the undersea city of films or the rubble of a fallen civilization, but a teeming metropolis of gleaming spires against a sky of an unnatural, almost neon, blue.

This was not the sky of earth, and even in her panic, Beatrice realized that the caverns and chambers where Calypso had brought them were not part of Atlantis ... they were merely a waystation between two worlds, maintaining a boundary and separation so their edges would not touch.

The boundary had been broken, perhaps by the Compass she carried. But she couldn't let it go, lest it be lost. The Artifact might hold the only possibility of passage back to their own reality.

"Girls!" Beatrice shouted. "Are you safe?"

"For the moment," Eliza called back. "I think the crevasse widened by about a metre, but our ledge is alright. What's happening up there?"

"One of the walls came down. I don't think the immortals will help us—maybe they've been cut off. But there's a city." Her gut twisted. "I think I need to go for help. There's nothing in this chamber that I can lower down to you."

"Go," Esme assured her. "We'll be alright. But please hurry."

"Be brave, my darlings," Beatrice told them, her heart breaking to let them out of her sight. "I won't be long."

She picked her way across the rubble and looked toward the fabled city, looking for anyone or anything that might help her girls. It was only now, as she poked her head through the opening, that she heard it.

The sounds of panic rising from the city.

Another tremor struck, and from her vantage point, she could see a bridge that connected two of Atlantis's concentric rings shudder and crumble.

The city was collapsing.

"Oh, God. What's happening?"

There was a disruption in the air next to her as the form of a man materialized. His hair was long, its waves blending together in shades of pewter and silver, tied neatly at his nape. His beard was full, but immaculately kept, almost as if it were carved in marble.

He regarded Beatrice with hazel eyes full of thought, but not kindness. It felt to her as though he could see every version of her at once: her past choices, her present fear, and her unrealized futures.

"The Compass is reunited. The fold between worlds cannot hold." His voice was devastatingly calm.

Beatrice clutched the Compass. "Tell me what to do! Help me save my children!"

The man inclined his head, considering each word with precision. "You may save them, but at a cost."

The earth trembled and Esme's cry pierced the air. "The ledge is crumbling!"

Outside the city, massive surging waves crashed down on the outer rings of Atlantis, scuttling fishing boats. A tower collapsed with a thundering crash, and the panicked screams of Atlanteans rose above the tumult.

"You will find that vines grow on the outside of this building. If you collect some, you can reach your daughters. You could take the Compass and flee back toward your boat. If you are expeditious, you can escape back to your world. But Atlantis will perish."

Beatrice shook her head violently as she watched another surge of water slam into the city. "No! You have to give me another option!"

His tone was measured. Impartial. As if either outcome weighed the same. "Destroy the Compass. Seal the Rift. Balance will be restored, and Atlantis will be saved." He paused, his eyes piercing into her very soul. "But the fold on the Earth-side will collapse. The sea will reclaim this in-between place. All who stand there—your husband, your daughters, your ship's crew—they will drown."

She nearly dropped the Compass.

"Mother? Mother, what's happening?" Eliza's voice rose from the chasm.

Beatrice broke into sobs. In the distance, she could see Atlanteans scrambling to find shelter, despite the futility. "No, no, no ..."

The ground shook again, and there was a crack from within the crevasse. Esme's and Eliza's voices rose in wordless panic.

"Mother, do something!" Esme pleaded. She had no idea ... no clue how high the stakes had become.

Beatrice looked out at the dying city, down to the Compass in her hands, and back toward her daughters—her world—trapped and afraid.

Her breath was ragged. "I'm sorry. I'm so, so sorry."

Not to the Council.

Not to Atlantis.

To her girls.

Images of Esme and Eliza flashed through her mind: Eliza and Esme arguing about the structural integrity of building block construction methods when they were tiny, Esme's stacks of sketches of her mother's face, Eliza's graduation speech, the two sisters huddled together in a rainy churchyard when they buried an empty casket for their brother ... Eliza and Esme had faced all of life together. Now they would face death together as well.

The thought brought Beatrice anguish and comfort at the same time.

She raised the Compass high above her head. The bearded man watched without emotion. Beatrice closed her eyes.

"I love you more than my life," she called Eliza and Esme. "I love you. But I will not let thousands die to save only us."

She slammed the Compass onto the stone floor, and the world exploded in a flash of white light.

When the blinding glare faded and Beatrice's eyes came back into focus, the chamber around her was whole. The cracks, rubble, and crevasse were gone. Eliza and Esme stood beside her ... unharmed, but horrified.

The collapsed wall which had revealed the city beyond was undamaged.

The Compass rested in the hands of the bearded man, unbroken. He stepped forward, still placid, but with a hint of respect in his ancient eyes.

"Hear me, members of the Council, champions, and observers. Hear the words of the Father of Knowledge! Beatrice Wren, grounded in the earth, forged in fire, and free as the air, has chosen not with the heart of a mother, but with the heart of a leader. She has chosen the many over the few. She has succeeded in the trial of sacrifice. Charmaine Andrews chose only to save her sisters. She is not ready to lead as a Champion must."

Charmaine's expression fell, not in anger, but in humiliation and heartbreak.

The pieces fell into place as Bea looked at her—it hadn't been real, none of it. It was an illusion, the third test. Charmaine had seen the same vision and failed because her loyalty for her sisters outweighed her sense of empathy for people she didn't know.

Though her head knew she had made the morally right choice, Beatrice felt heartsick with grief that she had chosen strangers over the ones she loved. She had won the challenge, but it didn't feel that way.

A hand gently touched her arm. Esme, her baby. Overwhelmed with emotion, Beatrice collapsed into the arms of her daughters.

"We're here, Mum. We're okay," Eliza murmured, wrapping her arms around her mother's waist.

"I thought I lost you," Beatrice wept. "I *chose* to lose you." She dissolved into tears.

"But you didn't lose us," Esme said, supporting her mother from the other side. "You did the right thing."

"This is leadership," the Father of Knowledge announced. "The courage to bear the unbearable for the sake of the world."

20

THE CHOICES WE MAKE

"*Pain is the price of choosing people over principles.*" Elias's words from almost two years ago resonated in Eliza's head as she sat feeling the weight of her defeat. Meanwhile, Beatrice explained to Simon and the others what had happened.

Eliza touched the gash on her cheek tenderly. "I hope it doesn't scar."

Esme held her hand. While Eliza was worried about her face, it was her defeat that stung more than anything. She'd been bested and worse, it had been at the hands of the brother who'd betrayed her. She'd lost. It'd forced her mother into a difficult decision and it didn't even bother Eliza that Beatrice hadn't chosen them. She'd done the right thing. *The needs of the many outweighed the needs of the few.* Spock had been right about that. She couldn't blame her mother. She blamed herself.

"So now what happens?" Simon asked. "We're still stuck here."

"The Father of Knowledge says there is a choice to be made." Beatrice paced, looking out over the bow of the ship that floated on the pool inside the grotto. Charmaine and her sisters stood on the beach, their backs to *The Pleiades* and its passengers.

"What choice?" Esme snapped.

"I guess we have to wait to find out," Beatrice said.

A chime rang and the force of it sent ripples over the mirror-still pool, rocking *The Pleiades* as the concentric rings spread over the surface of the water. Eliza rose, finding herself on the shore beside her mother and sister. Esme still held her hand. She felt her mother's fingers slip into her other.

The waters churned and the nymph and her army of merfolk rose from the depths, joining them as the Father of Knowledge appeared. Calypso made a nod of respect to him as the assembly came together.

"Calypso, you have challenged the Council of Seven. Your champions have defeated your opponents. You have a choice. What is your will?"

"I wish to return to my home. Atlantis is where I belong. I ask nothing else."

"And what is your will for the defeated challengers?"

"That they make their own choice," Calypso said, turning to Charmaine and her sisters. "Here, your betrayal may be judged harshly and your fate is not in your own hands. Or you may serve me in the land of your ancestors."

"Serve you? We are daughters of Atlantis. We are no one's servants." Charmaine's tone spoke of disdain. "*Better to reign in Hell than serve in Heaven*. I haven't done anything wrong. I'll take my chances here."

"Speak for yourself," Rhea retorted. "I've only seen a glimpse of Atlantis, and I want to know more."

Corrine moved to stand beside Rhea. "You said you wanted the Compass to find Atlantis so we could go back to the land of our people. Were you lying?"

"I said I wanted to *find* our ancestral homeland," Charmaine corrected her.

"But to what end?" Corrine asked, turning to Calypso and not waiting for an answer from her sister. "It would be an honor to serve in a land of such magnificence."

"So let it be," Calypso said. The same chime rang, upsetting the water that had gone still.

"What?" Charmaine's face twisted in anger. "You can't go with her. You're *my* sisters. I chose *you* over Atlantis, because family sticks together."

"Atlantis is where our family came from," Rhea snapped as she moved to stand behind Calypso. "It *is* our family. It's the family you turned your back on when you had a choice."

"But ..." Charmaine's face grew red as she stomped her foot in the wet sand at her feet, and the water beneath *The Pleiades* began to boil. "No! I will not allow this!"

"This was the price of the challenge," The Father of Knowledge pronounced judgement. "So it is to be." He turned to Eliza, Esme, and Beatrice. "The Council of Seven commend your courage, your wisdom, and your faith. Return, and take the Compass and its crystal, but be warned, as you seek and find such treasures, there is a price to be paid for its use. Wisdom will only carry you so far. Ensure courage does not turn into arrogance, and never let faith and fear be confused."

The water began to rise around their ankles. Calypso collected Rhea and Corrine, leaving Charmaine to protest, her anger nowhere close to diminished. "This is unacceptable!" she shouted. "I won't allow this!"

"Come on," Beatrice gathered up her girls. "Back to *The Pleiades*! Swim as fast as you can."

Eliza moved a half-beat slower than the rest of the group, but she stopped and turned back. "Come on!" She ignored Charmaine's protests and grabbed her, pulling her toward the water. "The cavern is flooding!"

Charmaine struggled, but the trembling in the cavern sent chunks of stalactites showering down. She fell in with the Wren girl and both of them dodged debris as they fought the surging waters to get to the back of *The Pleiades*. Simon and Baxter helped Beatrice and Esme onto the deck, while Mateo pulled Eliza out of the water. Charmaine was sucked under for a moment, but Nico dove in after her and pulled her back up, hoisting her up to Mateo and Baxter before hauling himself out of the water.

The Pleiades came about, turning hard to port as a whirlpool developed beneath them. "Grab onto something!" Captain Baxter got everyone to the center of the yacht, scrambling to reach the life jackets stored in the cockpit lazaret, handing them out as everyone filed into the salon. He made sure everyone had one on before he donned his own.

The din of the churning water and collapsing grotto grew deafening as the ship was borne aloft, breaking through into the sea above them, the ship rolling and turning upside down, and back upright as it broke the surface of the Mediterranean.

Salt water blinded Eliza. Esme's panicked cries echoed in her head until she realized she could draw in air. She pushed back the water from her eyes and blinked her vision clear, realizing she was sitting on the deck of *The Pleiades* under a brilliant sun.

"Is everyone okay?" Baxter's voice found her in her reverie. "Eliza? You okay?" He knelt in front of her.

"What happened?" she muttered, taking his hand so he could lift her up onto the seat nearby. "Where are my glasses?"

"I'm not really sure," the captain said, "but we're back where we belong."

"Eliza," Simon came to sit beside her, putting an arm around his oldest daughter. "Esme. Bea." He reached for the others as they came to sit beside Eliza. "We're safe." Eliza held her face in her hands, wracked with sobs, tears she couldn't control. She'd failed and it wasn't something she was accustomed to. Beatrice pulled her into her arms and held her.

"There's a boat!" Mateo shouted. Eliza glanced up, seeing the approaching vessel.

"We're saved," Bea patted her shoulder. "Dry your tears. We're okay."

"Nothing else is dry," Esme snarked.

"I'll go see if there are towels below deck that are dry." Amalie squeezed water from her hair as she started for the stairs.

"It's Phillip Thorpe!" Simon turned back, grinning. "Imagine that. I knew I liked that Yank."

Eliza stood, pushing off her mother's hand as she stepped up to see. Phillip stood on the bow, his hand raised. He spotted her and she could almost make out the grin that spread across his face. "Phillip," she muttered. "Phillip!"

"Looks like your braw lad came to save the day," Beatrice quipped. Eliza forgot her own worries, and ignored her mother's attempt at a Scottish accent.

When the boat neared, Mateo positioned the fenders along the hull. Baxter tossed over a line and Phillip caught it, twisting it onto the mooring cleat and bringing the two boats side by side. As soon as everything was secured, he leapt over to *The Pleiades*. Eliza was waiting for him, her arms open as he embraced her. He recoiled. "You're soaking wet."

"Now so are you," she managed, glancing at his damp shirt.

"I don't even care." He pulled her back into him, running a hand down her damp hair, pressing her head to his lips. "I've been worried sick."

"What are you even doing here?" Esme said. "I thought you had to go back to Pompeii?"

"I ran into someone," Phillip turned loose of Eliza. He turned as Elias stepped out of the wheelhouse on *Naxos*.

Beatrice sucked in a breath, and Eliza watched her mother go pale, her hand covering her mouth as she stood, trembling. Simon looked equally stunned. He turned to Phillip, and met Eliza's gaze.

"My son!" Beatrice called out, and was the first to move.

Elias joined them aboard *The Pleiades*, looking sheepish. "Mother."

"Oh!" she gasped, reaching for him, pulling him into her arms. "My son. We knew you were alive. But I don't think I truly believed it until this moment."

Elias embraced his mother and Eliza's heart broke as tears spilled down his face, realizing how badly she'd wanted that reunion. Not for herself, but for her parents. She couldn't imagine how awful it might be for a mother and father to think their son was dead.

Her mother shook with silent sobs. He lifted his gaze to his sisters, then to their father. When Beatrice turned him loose, he stepped toward Simon. "Father. I'm sorry I couldn't ..."

"None of that matters," Simon stuck his hand out. Elias hesitated. He took his father's hand. Simon gave him a stoic hand shake, then pulled him into his arms. "Welcome home, son."

Eliza glanced up at Phillip who put an arm around her. "You and my brother? How long have you been looking for us?"

"Several days," Phillip admitted. He leaned in and lowered his voice. "He's a bit of an ass, but I kinda like him."

Esme stepped in front of Phillip, her finger jabbing in the front of his damp shirt. "For the record, my sister doesn't need some knight in shining armor running around trying to save her," she snipped.

Phillip's head tilted and his brow lifted. "Kinda seems like she does."

"Oh, hell no." Esme shook her head. "This princess saves herself." She pointed at her sister. "And if she doesn't, I do."

Eliza started to get in the middle of the discussion until she saw Elias lock eyes with Charmaine who sat by watching the whole happy reunion with a sour expression chiseled into her face. "Charmaine," Elias said. "This is all your doing, isn't it?"

"Oh, sure, make me into the bad guy," she snapped.

"We'll take it up with Solan," Simon said, putting a hand on Elias's shoulder. "Bax? Is this craft functional, or do we need to commandeer my son's craft to get to shore?"

Baxter looked to Mateo. "We'll go see," he said. He hesitated. "Dr. Wren? Care to join us?"

Eliza hesitated. She'd been less than helpful the last time anyone asked her to help work on the ship, and she'd failed her challenge. She glanced at Elias, and locked eyes with him. "If you can spare me, Captain, I need a word with my brother. I think a family meeting is in order. We have a lot of things to work out."

"Fair enough," Baxter said, as Amalie returned from below deck with a stack of towels. "How is it down below?"

"Ship shape and in Bristol fashion," she mimicked a British accent. "Like nothing ever happened."

"In that case, I think everyone could benefit from a cuppa and a bite of something," Baxter suggested.

"I'm on it," she said. "And then I'll get started on dinner preparations."

"I'll go ..." Phillip started to go back over to the *Naxos*.

"Stay," Eliza said. "We might need a neutral witness to this conversation."

"I'm not sure I can be objective," he admitted. "I'm on your side."

"There are no sides when it comes to family," Eliza said. "Stay."

"Sounds like you're practically family already, old chap." Simon beamed.

"That's a conversation for later," Phillip smirked, a wry grin on his face.

"And not one for you and me," Simon stated. "That's between you and my daughter. She makes her own choices and she doesn't need my permission to do anything."

Eliza stood, her lower jaw fallen. Did her father just say what she thought he said? That was premature. They hadn't even had a proper first date.

"So noted, sir." Phillip nodded. He grinned at Eliza, and took her hand, moving to join the family in the salon.

Elias stopped and held out a hand to allow Phillip to pass. "After you, brother."

21

Debrief

Randall Greaves, the Order's illustrious and enthusiastic Archivist, sat behind his desk, his spectacles sliding precipitously down his nose. His stylus was poised above a recording slate that was conspicuously blank. It was the second time Eliza had seen him since returning from the Mediterranean, and she still wasn't quite sure Faraday had forgiven her for bringing him home from Randall's care.

The Archives, despite Randall's meticulous tidiness save for a few stray cat hairs, had always smelled faintly of dust and ink. The stacks, as he called them, and the vaults below were places where the Order kept things it did not fully understand but was not willing to destroy. Tall shelves lined the walls, the volumes bound in leather, vellum, and stranger materials that lacked easy categorization.

An Aegis containment crate holding the Midnight Tea Set lay on the floor beside Beatrice's chair.

"This is ... unusual," he began. "But given the circumstances of Charmaine's, um, uncertain future, I agree with Solan. I'm the right person to take down your situation report, even if I haven't done anything like this in nearly twenty-five years."

Beatrice folded her hands. Eliza sat straight-backed. Esme leaned against the edge of the desk, sketchbook tucked under one arm.

They told him what mattered.

Not every detail of *The Pleiades* developing a mind of its own—Randall would read the crew's statements later—but enough. The Compass. The Ruby Nautilus. Calypso's challenge. The trials and the Council of Seven. Charmaine's ambition. Atlantis.

Randall listened without interruption, his eyes wide, but his expression unreadable. He jotted down details in a cryptic shorthand as Tiberius, a stout orange tabby supervised from the top of an old metal filing cabinet, eyeing Eliza with disdain since she'd taken his new best friend home with her. Only when Beatrice spoke of the final trial did his pen still.

"There was a man," Beatrice said slowly. "One of the Council of Seven. Bearded, and older. He called himself 'Father of Knowledge.'"

Randall looked up at once. "Can you describe him in more detail?"

Before Beatrice could answer, Esme stepped forward and opened her sketchbook. She flipped to a page and turned it so Randall could see.

The drawing was precise and careful, not Esme's usual style. The lines were confident, but restrained. A bearded man in ancient Greek garb gazed out from the pencil sketch with deepset eyes that were grave, but not unkind.

Randall inhaled sharply. "That's not possible," he murmured. "Though I should probably quit saying that about anything to do with the Order."

Eliza frowned. "You recognize him."

"Yes," Randall answered. "I've seen him before. Not like this, but close enough." He rose and crossed to one of the shelves, practically skipping with excitement, returning a moment later with a folio. He opened it to a charcoal rubbing of a marble bust.

The resemblance was unmistakable.

"Herodotus," Randall said, grinning. "The Father of History. Or, as some of the older texts insist, Father of Knowledge."

Beatrice's breath caught. "He spoke as if he was judging me. As if ... he knew exactly what my choice would cost."

Randall nodded slowly. "That seems on-brand."

Bea hesitated, then continued. "At the end, after the illusion fell, he said something else. About me."

"What did he say?"

She closed her eyes, recalling the moment. "He said I was 'forged in fire, free as air, grounded in earth.' Or nearly that."

The room went very still.

Randall's hand tightened on the folio. "Say that again."

Beatrice repeated it as the girls nodded.

Randall set the folio on his desk and strode to the filing cabinet. After giving Tiberius an obligatory chin scratch—a payment for the gatekeeper—he opened a drawer and sifted through the folders until he found what he sought. He pulled out a printed piece of paper in a plastic sheet protector. "Remember this?"

Beatrice took the plastic from him. On one side, a crayon sketch in a childlike hand of birds, trees and people—"The Twelve Days of Christmas" as interpreted by a five-year-old Esme—and on the other side, a poem which carried echoes of the famous carol.

Randall pointed to one of the stanzas. "*Three queens of knowledge—earth, air, fire—/*

Nested beneath a shattered dome." He looked up now, eyes bright with recognition.

"The shattered dome," Beatrice breathed. "Atlantis."

Eliza leaned forward. "And the three queens?"

Randall made a sweeping gesture toward the Wren women, his grin widening. "You tell me!"

Esme spoke first. "Earth. That was Mother. Grounded. She didn't hesitate when she realized the loss of life."

Eliza swallowed. "Air ... clarity. Perspective. That's—" She stopped, then squared her shoulders. "That's me. Even if I failed my trial."

All eyes turned to Esme.

"Fire," Randall said. "Transformation. Catalyst."

Esme hugged herself, her smile reflecting something—not pride exactly, but something steadier. Purpose, perhaps.

"And my two turtle doves." Beatrice put a hand on each daughter's leg.

Randall bounced on the balls of his feet just a little. "*The doves fly not apart, nor tethered—/They are the bond. One sees the path, the other shields it.* Eliza and Esme," he nodded. "Sight and protection. Knowledge and guardianship. The Order has been waiting for you."

Silence stretched between them.

Beatrice sobered. "And then there's this." She pulled a tote bag out from under her chair and handed it to Randall.

He took it from her, a quizzical look on his face that morphed into shock when he beheld the bag's contents.

He reached in and pulled out the Compass with the Ruby Nautilus ensconced in the center. "Is this what I think it is?"

The three women nodded in unison.

"But how did you get it? It's supposed to be ... Oh, my! Did Charmaine steal this from the Vaults?"

"You know as well as I do, Randall, that even in her former position, Charmaine didn't have the security clearance to remove Artifacts from the

Vaults." Beatrice's tone was hard, but her eyes betrayed a hint of sorrow. "The Compass was onboard *The Pleiades.* Esme retrieved the Ruby."

"Onboard *The Pleiades*? But that means—" His brow grew troubled.

"It means Solan has some explaining to do. And now, if you'll indulge me, I'd like to accompany you to the Vaults and see this and the tea set are locked away properly."

Solan's office overlooked a grey sweep of London rooftops, the late afternoon flattening the city into slate and glass. Somewhere beneath the streets a few miles away, far below the hum of traffic and footfalls of Londoners and tourists alike, the Vaults lay sealed once more. The Compass had been returned to where it belonged.

Beatrice stood with her hands folded calmly before her. Simon remained beside her, silent and unyielding.

"The Compass is secure," Beatrice stated, her voice flat. "It's back in the Vaults. Randall logged the return himself."

Solan Virell nodded. "Good." He paused. "That was always my intention."

Simon's gaze sharpened and he bristled. "Your intention? Intentions don't move Artifacts away from their protected locations under the British Museum. You—"

A flicker of irritation crossed Solan's face. "Charmaine argued that it made sense to keep it aboard *The Pleiades*. That its presence would protect the yacht, the crew, the passengers ..." He looked pointedly at Simon, as if their safe return was evidence. "She was ... persuasive."

Beatrice met his eyes without blinking. "She was only persuasive because you wanted to believe her. We've been friends for a long time, Solan. So it falls to us to make you hear the truth, even if it's not pretty. 'The uglier the truth, the truer the friend,' as they say. Charmaine didn't care about the boat being safe. She wanted to find the Ruby and Atlantis. And she needed the Compass to do those things. She played on your vanity like a Stradivarius."

Solan exhaled and turned toward the window. "It's a fair cop. But it all worked out. No one was hurt."

"As far as we know," she pointed out. "That distinction matters."

The hush that followed was heavy with years of trust, shared history, and unspoken disappointment.

Simon broke the quiet. "What do you intend to do about Charmaine?"

Solan's shoulders tightened. "She's violated no written statute. Caused no documented harm. And she knows too much for us to simply sever ties."

"Which makes her dangerous," Simon observed.

The Grand Aegis's jaw flexed. "Charmaine is ambitious, brilliant, and convinced she knows the Order better than anyone. She might be right about that."

"And?" Beatrice asked.

"And," Solan continued, lowering his voice, "she's in possession of information that would be ... inconvenient if mishandled."

Beatrice inclined her head. "This is not merely a disciplinary issue. It's a consequence."

For the first time, Solan looked truly tired. "I'll handle it."

"I sincerely hope you do," Bea replied, "because next time, we may not be standing in an office discussing what *might* have happened."

A gentle, even hesitant, knock at the door interrupted them. Solan turned toward it, grateful for the interruption. "Yes?"

An assistant stepped inside, pale and unsettled. "Apologies, sir. There's been a development."

Solan sighed. "What is it?"

"It's Ms. Andrews, Grand Aegis," the assistant said, forcing himself to look the Grand Aegis in the eye. "She failed to report to debrief this morning. Her London flat is empty. Her access card registered one final use to access the building last night and then it went dark."

Simon's expression hardened. "Where is she now?"

"We don't know, Grand Aegis."

Solan closed his eyes briefly. When he opened them, his composure had returned, but it was brittle now, stretched thin.

"That will be all. Thank you."

The door closed softly behind the assistant as he scuttled out.

Simon and Beatrice exchanged a look.

Some things could not be returned to the Vaults.

22

Epilogue

All That Remains

Elias sat in the bistro just across the street from the headquarters of the Aegis Order. The coffee was as bitter as his mood, but it chuffed off the chill of a rainy London day. He hadn't expected to be summoned back into the fold, or to meet Solan with open arms. He still had a long way to go in winning back his family's trust, but the tentative détente seemed *enough*, for now.

He was looking forward to dinner with his sisters so they could begin building the foundation of any future relationship they might have. He wanted so badly to have peace after all these years. But it didn't change how he felt about Solan, or his questionable methods. A man had to answer for his actions. People had been lost because of his failure as Grand Aegis, and their lives were worth more than being written off as collateral damage.

Until leadership changed, his status with the Order wouldn't either. He couldn't go back to the Obsidian Covenant, but if he was being honest with himself, he didn't want to. So, he knew what he *didn't* want. Now, he just had to decide where to go from here.

He had options. He had all the education required to teach at Oxford, if there was a post he might find of interest. He could travel abroad, if he so chose. Hell, he could be a tour guide at the Tower of London if nothing else. He had saved some money, and didn't need to work right away, but occupation might be the best thing for him.

The bells of St. Paul's brought him from his musings, trying to imagine himself lecturing to new trainees on the arcane puzzles and relic mechanisms, but Aegis would never allow that.

"Sixpence for your thoughts," a soft voice drew his attention. He looked up to see Charmaine standing beside the empty chair across from him.

"I didn't expect to see you here," he sat up, but held out a hand indicating she should sit. "Would you like a coffee? A gin and tonic perhaps?"

"No," she muttered, not meeting his gaze. "Thank you."

Elias studied her long lashes that only accented the dark circles under her eyes. She looked like a woman who hadn't had a good night's sleep in weeks. "How did your meeting go with Solan?"

"It didn't," she said. She spoke to him in a soft tone she didn't use with others, certainly not Solan. She'd always let Elias see a more vulnerable side. That comfortable familiarity wasn't unwelcome. In truth, he had missed it. "I was scheduled in his office at the end of day, but—"

Elias winced. "That's usually when the hatchet falls in most corporate jobs, you know."

"This is not news to me, Elias." She sat stiffly, her eye going to his half empty espresso cup. She folded her hands in her lap, her ankles crossed. She wasn't dressed in the sleek pencil skirts and silk blouses she might normally wear. Instead, she wore a track suit under a summerweight rain jacket. He realized he'd never seen her in anything so casual.

He could see the strain of her situation in the faint creases around her dark brown eyes. An old but faint sense of sympathy returned and for a moment he almost felt guilty for how things had ended between them. Charmaine was also dealing with the loss of her sisters. They had turned on her, and left her behind. He'd known what it was like to be separated from his own sisters. But at least he still had hope.

"I've been fretting for days trying to think of what to say. Should I argue in my own defense, or graciously tenure my resignation? It's over, I know."

Elias felt a familiar ache in his chest. Once upon a time, she'd been the woman he loved. *His first*. He built a future for them in his head without even realizing it. Long gone were the quiet dinners, long walks in the park—hand-in-hand. He realized now she'd used him as a stepping stone. She wanted to advance her career. He was a Wren, one of the most powerful families within the Order. She might have had plans that when he took his place in leadership, she would be by his side. He was never anything more than an asset.

"What will you do now?" Her question caught him off guard. That was the same question *he* wanted to ask *her*.

"Oh," Elias sat up, fidgeting with the saucer and cup as if that might buy him time to come up with an answer. "I suppose that remains to be seen. What about you?"

"I wasn't much older than you were when I joined the Order. Solan offered me a tremendous opportunity with a promise of advancement that never quite worked out. All these years, I've never been more than a secretary to him. No matter how hard I worked, no matter how loyal or how clever I could be, I was just his *girl Friday*, and would never be more than that. Certainly not now."

"You had a role that afforded you access to power, and you used it. That's why Solan had the Compass on his personal yacht, isn't it? You suggested it, and he ran with it."

Charmaine hesitated at that remark, her jaw hanging slack as she considered him a moment. "Solan made his own decisions."

"True."

"I was always useful, but it made me invisible."

"You were manipulating him because he had something you wanted," Elias called her out. He'd realized she was playing him now. But he wasn't some school boy with a crush. Not anymore. "You've always been quite good at that."

Her expression turned from one of surprise to one of resentment. "Men of power are easy to control, at least to a certain degree."

"What about me? Was I easy to control?"

"You never had power," she stated flatly. It was true, but a burn none the less.

"Proximity to power," Elias offered. Yes, he was a Wren and he could have been something great within the Order, had he agreed with their ethics—their tactics.

"Perhaps." Charmaine was never one to bow out of an argument, so clearly she wasn't trying to pick one.

Elias wasn't sure what he wanted out of this conversation. The love they had once shared could never be rekindled. Then he realized what her game was now.

"You don't want respect. You want permission to stop pretending that you care about any of this."

His words stung; he could see it in her eyes. Still, she held her poise and sharpened her expression. "You always believed in me, even when no one else did." Her hand stretched across the table to rest on his arm.

His gaze lifted from her hand to her eyes, in challenge. She drew back her hand as he spoke, "I see you for what you've always been. A patient viper, waiting for the right moment to strike."

"We aren't that different, you and I." Charmaine swallowed hard. "But I truly did love you, Elias."

He balled his fist on the table, and bit his lip. He took a deep breath, then softened, relaxing into his chair, knowing she would never change. "If I ever thought I felt anything for you, Charmaine, now I know."

"Know what?" She tilted her head and lowered her voice, as if encouraging him into something that could never be.

"This is what it's like when love dies." Her mouth fell open and she gasped, as if wounded by the truth in his words. He wasn't angry. He wasn't hurt. He was *done*. And now, she knew it. "Your greatest flaw lies in believing that control equals safety. I'm afraid you'll find that nowhere is safe when you are *a woman without a country*, so to speak."

Charmaine drew in a deep breath, and rose. "I guess this is goodbye forever, then."

She picked up her tote and Elias realized how full it was. Files, papers, trinkets from her office, and a bouquet of flowers that were refreshed daily and sat on her desk next to her phone.

Charmaine had no intention of going back to the Order.

She wasn't about to face Solan or accept whatever judgement he had in mind.

Coward.

Elias looked forward to the reckoning that was coming between himself and the Grand Aegis. Solan would hear what he had to say. It wasn't going to be pretty and neat. It was going to be blunt and brutal.

Elias watched her as she pulled her scarf over her head and dashed out into the drizzling evening, hailing a cab. She glanced back as she got in, then closed the door behind her and was gone from his life. *Goodbye forever, then.*

Elias glanced at his watch. It was time. He rose and slipped out of the bistro as the grey day faded into a greyer night.

He knew Solan's habits all too well. Elias made his way to the rendezvous spot he'd selected. He waited in the deep charcoal shadows, his navy coat and his grudge melding him into the darkness.

Solan Virell—lauded, respected, and hypocritical bastard that he was—stepped confidently from the hidden door at the back of St. Paul's Cathedral and gazed at the cloudy London sky.

He didn't even seem to care if people saw him. The Grand Aegis took a deep breath and headed for his car up the block.

Elias, taking his darkness with him, followed.

EXCERPT: THE HANGED MAN

BOOK 3 OF THE MANIFEST DESTINY SERIES

August 3

New Orleans, LA, USA

Alligators and snakes weren't the only monsters lurking in the swamps of Louisiana. Practitioners of dark magic used the tangled bayous for centuries. Dark magic thrived in places where law and light were shunned. The swamp had always been willing to conceal secrets that needed to stay buried. When it finally gave something back, it did so without mercy.

Bodies floated to the surface. Hidden treasures emerged in times of drought. Sometimes no one knew how secrets re-emerged, but the consequences were always the same. Magic—whether for good or ill—always came at a cost.

The tarot card didn't look dangerous sitting behind glass in a cramped metaphysical shop off Chartres Street, nestled between hand-painted saints and mass-produced candles. But curses rarely announce themselves.

Isolde Sinclair tried to mask the thrum of excitement that washed through her as she studied it, and tried to determine if it was genuine. The antiquarian and occult artifact broker knew—if she could validate it—it would be of interest to her old friend Maelis Varrow back in England.

Maelis was an occultist herself, interested in certain artifacts but they were few and far between. It had been nearly a decade since Isolde had spoken to her, but she recalled a discussion about the tarot card.

The Hanged Man belonged to the Major Arcana.

At first glance, the card was unassuming, though the artwork was exquisite. A man hung upside down from a wooden frame, one ankle bound, the other leg bent behind him, almost in a casual cross. His hands were hidden behind his back. Not bound, but restrained by choice, or by faith. A faint halo surrounded his head, suggesting insight gained through suffering, rather than defeat.

But there was something wrong with this card.

The wood wasn't a gallows. It was a living tree, its bark etched with symbols worn smooth by time—older than tarot itself. The man's face showed no peace, no enlightenment. His eyes were open, fixed on something beyond the viewer. It was as if he understood exactly who had betrayed him—and why. The rope at his ankle wasn't fiber, but something darker, braided in a way that suggested hair, sinew or prayer threads soaked in blood.

In the traditional tarot, *The Hanged Man* signified sacrifice, suspension and surrender. It was the moment when forward momentum stopped and a different perspective was forced upon the seeker. It was the card of waiting, of voluntary loss in service of a greater truth. Upright, it spoke of transformation through patience. Reversed, it warned of martyrdom without meaning, of betrayal mistaken for destiny.

This version carried no such ambiguity. Here, sacrifice wasn't chosen. It was forced.

Scholars might argue the image echoed older rites, perhaps Odin hanging from the World Tree to gain knowledge of runes—bound and displayed as offerings to chthonic gods. Hanging between life and death so spirits might speak through him. Some whispered that the card predated Europe entirely—that it reflected rituals carried across time and tides, rewritten again and again until they resurfaced under the guise of a simple fortune-teller's tool.

The Hanged Man did not ask what must be given, instead, it demanded to know who dared wield it. Isolde didn't dare so much for herself, but the handsome finders fee Maelis offered up forced a necessary alliance between the freelance artifacts broker and the leader of the Obsidian Covenant.

She also knew there would be others seeking the artifact, and while she didn't like to be rushed, she also didn't hesitate to step into the shop and make inquiry.

"Hey, baby." The man behind the counter spoke in a Cajun patois. "How ya'll are t'day? Mighty hot out der." He dressed in black robes with red embroidered trim, dark eyeliner smeared down his face, giving him a morose appearance. Clearly, it was for the benefit of the tourists. Not all occultists looked like goth teenagers.

Isolde brushed back a lock of copper hair, swiping at the bead of sweat that threatened to show cracks in her carefully presented façade. "Good afternoon," she spoke with a measured tone, her accent carrying the soft French vowels sharpened by Scottish consonants, a subtle reminder that she didn't belong just to one country. Her mixed heritage, and her family's constant relocation between Scotland and France had given her a much broader perspective of the world. "I couldn't help but notice this tarot card in the window. Can you tell me more about it?"

"Ah yeah, baby. You gots a good eye." He rose from his stool and moved to the case, unlocking it with a delicate skeleton key on a rubber spiral band on his wrist. He held it by the edges, and only as he brought it to the velvet mat on the counter in front of her did she realize it was tucked into a plastic sleeve.

Isolde leaned over and studied it. "Do you know where it came from?" she asked.

The clerk hesitated a fraction too long, then smiled. It was a practiced expression he must have reserved for only the most curious of customers who wanted atmosphere more than truth.

"Depends on who ya'll ask," he drawled. "Folks say it turned up in the nineteenth century. Old New Orleans family. One of those involved in a most unpleasant event."

"Unpleasant." Isolde echoed.

He lowered his voice. "Madame LaLaurie."

Of course.

"The fella dat sold it to me said dey were cataloguing effects pulled from a sealed trunk found in de attic of de LaLaurie house, before Nick Cage bought it, dat is." He paused only a moment, leaning in to continue spinning his tale. "Dey was other tings in dat trunk. Letters, jewelry, personal effects. Dey was also voodoo trinkets. The usual horrors. Dis card was tucked inside a book—no title, no author. Just the card. Folks say it was used in private readings. Dark ones. But also in punishment rituals. It be a warning card."

Isolde allowed him his drama, but she knew better. "LaLaurie wasn't known for divination." The woman he spoke of was known for her cruelty. Torture of her servants. She was a blackheart of the worst kind.

The clerk shrugged. "People like her tend t' hide who dey really are. Some say she had a woman come by de house—practice voodoo, read cards, curse enemies. Others say de card was used on servants. She played on dey superstitions t' teach obedience."

"And you believe that?"

He spread his hands beside the card. "Don't matta' what I believe. Dis is N'awlins. If sometin' is old and ugly enough, it gets pinned on Madame LaLaurie ..."

"Or Marie LaVeau," Isolde added.

The man shrugged, drawing back his hands. "Either one. Makes it easy to sell."

Isolde smiled faintly. "I don't suppose it has documentation?"

"Lost," he said, too quickly. "Lot of t'ings were lost in Katrina."

Yes. It was easy to blame the worst hurricane in decades. The story, though, was neat. Too neat. This card had been hidden on purpose.

"How much are you asking for it?"

"Card like dis is worth a lot."

"But how much are you selling it for?"

"Boss lady has it listed at $5,000."

"And the cock-and-bull story comes free?" she challenged.

"The myth is as important as the card." He stood and moved to put it back in the glass case. "If you know anyt'ing about magic, baby, you know dat its the history that gives a relic like dis its power."

"It's *true* history," she corrected. "Yes. But without documentation, you can't prove it."

He locked the case and returned to his stool. "Den I guess you don't wan' it."

"I'll give you fifty dollars. Cash." Isolde crossed her arms but held his gaze. "And that's me being generous."

"You're missin' some zeros, baby."

"Zeroes require documentation," she said. "I'll be back tomorrow. Perhaps something will turn up."

"Don't bank on it."

Isolde turned and calmly walked out of the shop. At that price, the card wasn't going anywhere. She had time.

Jared sat in the empty shop the rest of the day, sending a text message to his manager explaining the exchange with the customer, letting her know she might want to be here tomorrow when the woman returned. At nine o'clock he rose from his stool, locked the front door and flipped the "OPEN" sign over to read "CLOSED". Then he went through and made sure all the incense burners were snuffed out. He tidied up a few shelves, and double checked the case where the card was secured. Then he made his way to the back door and stepped out into the dark alley where tourists didn't dare venture. His bright yellow moped was parked behind a dumpster, the rancid perfume of the French Quarter heavy in the muggy night air.

He hopped on the bike and flipped the main switch to the *on* position. He squeezed the brakes then turned the key in the ignition until it clicked. Then pressed the start button with his thumb.

Nothing happened.

The engine didn't even try to fire up. "Jeezus, baby. Don't do dis t' me," he muttered, trying again.

That was when the footsteps came.

He turned, mouth open to speak, and the world collapsed into pain. Something hard struck the side of his head. He stumbled, the bike toppling over as he slid down the wall into the damp puddle. A blur of shadow loomed over him. It moved slowly, patiently. Efficient. Gloved fingers closed around his arm, cool and unhurried, sliding the coiled band with the key off his wrist. He caught the assailant's hand, twisting, fighting the spinning world for a moment's clarity, trying to get a look at a face, or to stop the inevitable.

A boot caught him between the ribs, and another blow to the head followed. He collapsed, hard, his head striking the concrete step into the shop. A wave of nausea spread through him, and his grip released as he faded into oblivion.

Two Days Later

Café Du Monde, New Orleans

Morning came softly in New Orleans. This was the hour when the clientele at Café Du Monde were almost exclusively locals. The tourists usually puked out by two or three am, and the few folks that sat around him as the sun broke over the river were there to grab a quick bite before they headed off to work or school.

"You got powdered sugar all over you, baby." Chantal, his waitress, grinned a big toothless grin. Phillip glanced down at his black t-shirt, frosted in the snow-like confection. "You need another cup of cafe au lait, hon?"

He brushed at his shirt but only succeeded in making it worse. "No. I've still got a two mile run back to the hotel."

"Where you from, baby?"

"Originally, Chicago," he said. "But I'm a bit of a vagabond these days."

"World traveler? Adventure seeking?"

"Traveling salesman, actually." It was easier than telling people he was an antiquities acquisitions archeologist for a secret society. He wasn't here for work, though he was looking for something.

"Well, I hope you get outta here before the hurricane makes landfall," she suggested.

"I was just reading in the paper it looks like it's going to turn and head to Florida," he had the *New Orleans Times-Picayune* spread out on the table beside his breakfast.

"Uh huh," she snorted. "And I'm in the running for Miss Louisiana. Dat newspaper ain't been right about a hurricane since 1964. My rheumatism never misses."

"That's hardly fair," Phillip observed. "Three years before Hurricane Katrina, reporters for the *Picayune* warned that the *big one* would hit New Orleans one day, and that it would submerge the city." And it had.

"Every blind squirrel finds a nut someday," she chuckled, and collected his empty plate and cup, wiping away the last of the powdered sugar from the table, and leaving him to enjoy his newspaper in peace. "Enjoy the Big Easy, baby."

He flipped the paper back to the front page, now prepared for the bad news portion of the program. The story that caught his eye was buried halfway down the page.

LOCAL SHOP CLERK FOUND DEAD—OCCULT ARTIFACT MISSING

That couldn't be good.

According to the article, it was a single tarot card, believed to be connected—according to their preliminary investigation, most likely online forums and local amateur treasure-hunters—to a long-forgotten treasure hunt game outlined in a 1960s book called ***X Marks The Spot: A Game for Modern Treasure Hunters*** by a New Orleans entrepreneur. The book encouraged readers to explore the city and surrounding bayous, promising hidden prizes for those clever or persistent enough to follow the clues. Most had dismissed it as a publicity stunt.

Phillip's fingers tightened on the paper as he turned back to the third page where the story continued. The article quoted a police spokesperson calling the tarot connection "pure speculation fueled by internet chatter and local legend". No suspects had been named. No motive had been established. The card itself was identified as *The Hanged Man*.

Thorpe lowered the paper and stared out over Jackson Square, where the fog rose like spectral ghosts. A shiver washed over him, despite the heat.

He knew better. Some puzzles were designed to conceal and never reveal. And when they did, it wasn't just a game.

www.ingramcontent.com/pod-product-compliance
Lightning Source LLC
LaVergne TN
LVHW040218110826
845146LV00005B/1338

9798999079992